CAUGHT!

Slocum shoved his Colt Navy back into the cross-draw holster and moved toward the barracks, darting from shadow to shadow. He finally sidled up to the barracks, his back against the cold wood planking. Just above him on the roof squatted the man responsible for giving him and Evangeline such a turn. He saw the man's boots poking over the edge.

Still wary, Slocum moved to one side and chanced a quick look up. A slow smile crossed his face. He had been right to be so cagey. Only a pair of boots rested on the roof. The man who had worn them was trying to get away.

Slocum drew his pistol and went in the other direction. He stood under a drainpipe as a man scampered down it. When the man's bare feet touched the top of a water barrel, Slocum jammed his pistol into the small of the man's back.

"Move and I'll cut you in half . . ."

OTHER BOOKS BY JAKE LOGAN

JAKE LOGAN

DESOLATION POINT

B

BERKLEY BOOKS, NEW YORK

DESOLATION POINT

A Berkley Book / published by arrangement with
the author

PRINTING HISTORY
Berkley edition / March 1991

ISBN: 0-425-12615-3

A BERKLEY BOOK® TM 757,375
Berkley Books are published by The Berkley Publishing Group,
200 Madison Avenue, New York, New York 10016.
The name ''BERKLEY'' and the ''B'' logo
are trademarks belonging to Berkley Publishing Corporation.

PRINTED IN THE UNITED STATES OF AMERICA

10 9 8 7 6 5 4 3 2 1

1

"Your hat, sir," said the butler. John Slocum silently handed the frozen-faced servant his silk top hat and then carefully peeled off his white linen gloves that didn't quite fit his large hands. He casually tossed them into the hat and walked off without a backward glance. All around him rose the majesty of San Francisco's finest private club. On the walls hung Gobelin tapestries. Marble tables lined the walls under the occasional gilt-edged mirror. The long marble floor stretched toward the back of the structure, an invitation to excess.

The opulence was as it should be. The Union Club catered only to San Francisco society's finest. Slocum kept his face impassive as he walked among the rich and famous of the city, trying to ignore the way his fancy suit pinched in some places and bagged in others. Leland Stanford sat at a corner table and talked earnestly with a small man sporting muttonchop whiskers turning to gray. Slocum had heard of the

railroad magnate and knew he was probably figuring out
some way of foreclosing on a farmer's land to gain right-
of-way for his Central Pacific line.

Across the room a small group of men chatted casually.
Slocum recognized two as leading San Francisco bankers
and the others as politicians. What unholy deals they were
carving out wouldn't be felt for weeks or months—but they
would affect thousands of lesser mortals. These were the
people surrounding Slocum this night.

He moved through the crowd and stopped at the long
teakwood bar imported at great expense from Shanghai. The
polish job was so good the reflection from it hurt his eyes.

"Your pleasure, sir?" asked the barkeep.

"Whiskey, neat," Slocum said. When he knocked back
the shot, he relished the way it burned like the very sun and
slid smoothly down his throat. No trade whiskey, this. The
Union Club served only the finest as befitting its clientele.

Slocum had worked hard to enter the huge carved oak
doors tonight. He had been in the city fewer than a dozen
days when he was hired as a bodyguard by a shipping
magnate. It hadn't been Slocum's fault that the man was
gunned down by highbinders on the wharf before he could
examine the newest China clipper he had purchased. And
if Slocum hadn't taken the man's wallet in way of payment,
someone else would have slipped it from the man's inner
pocket.

In that wallet lay five hundred dollars. More than this, it
held a simple white card with raised printing on it admitting
its bearer to the Union Club.

If Slocum wanted to make a real killing in San Francisco,
it was here among the rich. He motioned for another drink
as his keen green eyes studied the gaming tables. Roulette
wasn't his game. It was pure chance and the odds favored
the house. Blackjack was better, but Slocum intended to
turn his five hundred dollar stake into thousands. To do that
he needed a high stakes poker game.

The lush Oriental carpeting smothered the footfalls of the

men moving toward a green-felt-covered table at the far side of the room. More and more club members drifted toward the three players at the table. Slocum couldn't help wondering if this might be the game that would make him rich. He had yet to see any one of the really well-to-do who knew the odds at a game of poker. If anything, they played as if they felt guilty about having so much money and just wanted to give it away.

"Sir," came the soft voice from behind the bar. "I wouldn't get involved with them, if I were you."

Slocum looked at the barkeep and decided the man was sincere. Slocum smiled crookedly and said, "Then it's a good thing you're not me. That's the richest game in this club."

"Oh, yes sir, it is that," the barkeep said. Slocum studied the man more carefully. The bartender knew when to keep his mouth shut. He had said his piece and been put in his place. Slocum was just a little worried at the expression on the barkeep's face.

It said he knew a sucker when he saw one—and Slocum was it.

This didn't keep Slocum from joining the crowd around the table and watching a few hands of seven card stud being dealt. For a few minutes he thought the barkeep might have been right. Large denomination greenbacks changed hands constantly, pot after pot.

Slocum pushed the amounts of money being won and lost from his mind. That wasn't the way to play poker. What about the three men at the table? Did they seem to be the kind of players to lose to John Slocum because he knew the odds and they didn't?

Yes!

He moved with the crowd toward the table and listened to what the others were saying. He kept his peace until a woman wearing far too much makeup asked him, "I don't understand the game. Why is the one with the three eights losing to the other man?"

"The man in the silk cravat," Slocum said, eyeing the huge diamond stickpin holding the cravat in place, "has a straight." He saw that the woman didn't understand. "He has five cards in sequence."

"Oh," she said in a low voice, showing she had no notion what was going on. She watched for a few seconds, then went to the bar. Slocum saw the barkeep pour her another drink and engage in some light banter.

The barkeep's advice gnawed at the back of his mind. If you sat down at a poker table and didn't identify the sucker immediately, *you* were the sucker.

Did that apply when all three of the others looked ripe for the plucking? The players got progressively drunker and made worse and worse bets. The only reason it didn't matter was that they were equally drunk and equally stupid. Slocum watched one man bluff another's three of a kind—and lose. The man with the red silk cravat and diamond stickpin folded with two pair, kings over tens, not a bad hand at seven card stud. Neither of the others had anything close to matching that. One had a bust hand and the other a pair of fours.

This was Slocum's game. He saw three suckers.

"Gentlemen," he said, "is there room for another at the table?"

One looked away, not even aware he was being spoken to. The man with the silk cravat silently pointed to an empty chair. Slocum smiled and sat down, acutely aware of how tight his pants were. He had rented the black swallowtail suit for the evening. His usual trail wear wouldn't have gotten him inside, even with the membership card he had taken from his former employer.

Slocum studied the three more closely now that he was in the game. The one with the silk cravat was the least drunk. He also seemed to have the smallest idea of how to bet. A man sitting ramrod straight, in spite of knocking back drink after drink, had a European look about him. The monocle dangling from a black grosgrain ribbon at his lapel added to Slocum's impression that he was a foreigner. The third man struggled to keep from falling out of his chair.

The biggest stack of chips and greenbacks was in front of him.

The play began. Slocum accepted a drink when it was brought but sipped slowly. He wasn't going to lose concentration when so much rode on his clear thinking. The pasteboard cards slipped off the deck with soft whispering sounds that came to his ears as the promise of money.

And it worked that way. He won small pots at first, but he had been right in his appraisal of the men. They were rich and didn't know a thing about seven card stud. Slocum bluffed—and won. Slocum had invincible hands—and won. No matter what he did, he won.

He had just raked in a pot containing several thousand dollars when a hand on his shoulder distracted him.

He looked at it. The long, slender feminine fingers had never seen a day's work. The nails were expensively manicured and the diamond ring on her finger was large enough to knock out his eye. He followed the hand back to a trim wrist where a gold bracelet dangled.

Turning, he looked up at the lovely woman behind him. A small smile danced at her lips. He wondered if he had ever seen anyone more beautiful in his life. Slocum guessed that he must have, but he couldn't remember when. The subtle fragrance of her perfume made his nostrils flare.

From the top of her brunette head all the way down to the floor he saw only perfection.

"You're winning," she said in a soft, lilting voice.

"I seem to be," Slocum said. If this was a club whore, the Union Club definitely went first class. But Slocum doubted it. There was nothing in the expensive jewelry or clothing or bearing that said she was anything but her own woman.

"Quit now. You have plenty."

"You're not quittin', you little pipsqueak," grumbled the drunkest of the three at the table. "You got a couple grand of my money. I want to get it back." He pounded the table. Hundred dollar chips danced. A stack of fifty dollar greenbacks toppled and fell, one fluttering to the floor. The man never noticed.

The man across from Slocum, the one with the silk cravat, said, "He's right. You got a lot of our money."

"Quit," came the woman's whisper.

Slocum had to evaluate what was going on. He was able to win endless amounts of money from these three. If anything, they were even more inept now than they had been earlier. Strong drink coupled with loss made them more reckless. And the woman, as beautiful as she was, proved only a small lure. If she was after his winnings, as Slocum thought most likely, she'd want him even more after he had cleaned out the men at the poker table.

"Another hand or two," he allowed.

The woman sighed deeply. Her hand left his shoulder and she walked off. This startled Slocum. If she was a gold digger, she would have stayed with him. He had won. He'd win more, *lots* more.

The two hole cards were useless to Slocum, as was the first up card. He folded rather than play out the hand. The next hand went the same way. The men grumbled but took the small amounts Slocum was putting back into the pot.

Slocum counted his earnings. He had over four thousand dollars stacked in front of him. Not a bad return on five hundred dollars he had stolen from a dead benefactor. But there was more to be had. More than he had ever seen in his life. On the table must be close to twenty thousand dollars. And it wasn't his—not yet.

The next hand was all he could have wanted. His two hole cards were diamonds. The first one up: another diamond. He bet heavily. The second card up: another diamond. He was close to his flush. The man with the monocle checked, but the drunk upped the bet two thousand on suspiciously bad cards. The man with the silk cravat folded.

Slocum's next card was a disappointment. A club. But he kept the pressure on. He had a chance of winning, a good one. The next card was another club, giving him a pair of tens to fall back on.

The last hole card dropped onto the table. Slocum had to fight to keep from showing his elation. He had gotten his flush. Five diamonds. Nothing the remaining two players had on the table would beat this, not the way they had played.

"I'm feeling lucky," said the European with the monocle. "I bet an additional two thousand dollars."

Slocum didn't have it. He had bet everything, but he wasn't turning his back on a flush. Not in this game.

"Will you accept my marker to call you?" Slocum asked.

The man with the silk cravat said, "I assume you are a gentleman, and gentlemen do not welsh on bets."

Slocum scribbled out his IOU and tossed it into the pot. "I have a flush. This is sufficient to win, I believe." He reached for the pot, only to have a curiously steady hand reach out and stop him.

"Gunther hasn't shown you his cards yet," the drunk who had dropped out earlier said.

Slocum's gut twisted and turned. The man was nowhere near as drunk as he had seemed. The room spun around him. He didn't have to see the European's cards to know that they did not favor John Slocum.

"Four nines beats your flush," the man with the monocle said. "It is a good thing all three of my hole cards were the same, eh?" He raked in the money, including Slocum's IOU.

"Let's make arrangements to pay, shall we? You owe Gunther two thousand dollars."

Slocum didn't have the money. All he had brought with him, the five hundred dollars, had been lost, also. Twenty-five hundred dollars lost on just one hand of cards.

"You three do this act often?" Slocum asked. The awful truth had just come to him. He had thought the three were the suckers. They were in cahoots. No matter which of them won, all three would split the winnings. That tripled their chance of winning.

All they had needed was an easy mark, and it had been John Slocum this evening.

"We are friends who enjoy a game at our club, nothing more," said the one Slocum had thought the drunkest. There wasn't a hint of slur in his words now. Whatever he had been drinking, it wasn't the potent whiskey served from the bar.

"I believe the gentleman is saying that he isn't able to pay," the one with the cravat said. "Can it be that you are not a gentleman?"

The coldness of the words told Slocum he would be found floating facedown in San Francisco Bay with the morning tide unless he came up with the money he had lost. He stiffened, as if affronted. He moved for the small derringer he carried in a vest pocket.

A hand on his elbow stopped him.

"Oh, really, you can't believe *he* is a deadbeat. You men. I do declare, you are the silliest things."

Slocum's ally was the brunette. She had returned and kept him from spilling blood on the fancy Union Club carpeting.

"Are you guaranteeing his losses?" The feral gleam in the man's eye spoke more of carnal lust than greed.

"I surely am. He and I are old friends, aren't we?"

Slocum could only nod. He was getting caught up in a situation beyond his control. He looked around and saw large, well-armed men inconspicuously positioned at the doors. The bouncers would never let him escape without a hard fight. He had been blinded by the club's elegance and hadn't seen the harder edge to it when he had entered.

"When might we be able to collect?" the man asked.

"Certainly not at this instant," the woman said. "I come here every evening to socialize with my friends. Tomorrow evening at this hour would be sufficient, wouldn't it?"

Slocum nodded again. He didn't trust himself to speak.

"How do we know—" started the European.

"Really, Gunther," interrupted the man with the cravat. "You malign the woman's integrity. But these Germans are such sticklers for protocol. We do not doubt your willingness to pay, but we would need collateral."

"Indeed," the lady said, slightly irritated at this. "Very well. Will this suffice until tomorrow?" She pulled the diamond ring from her finger. Gunther almost snatched it from her hand.

"We will be expecting you, Miss—"

"Dunbar. Evangeline Dunbar. Everyone here knows me. Oh, look, there's Leland. Wait, Leland! Oh, dear, he left without saying good-bye to me. How positively naughty of him."

Slocum saw the railroad magnate stalking from the room. Something had angered him and he wasn't likely to stop for pleasantries, even with a woman as lovely as Evangeline Dunbar.

"Very well," said the man with the silk cravat, "but you realize that we must garner some small interest on this debt." He was torn between staring at the beautiful woman and the glittering ring Gunther held up to the light.

"Yes, it must be considered a loan," spoke up the European who had supposedly won the money. The way the other two spoke for him, it was obvious they split the take.

"Ten percent is not out of the question," said the fake drunk. "Tomorrow evening. Twenty-two hundred dollars."

"That seems a bit much, doesn't it?" Evangeline turned to Slocum and batted her long eyelashes. Her brown eyes were deep pools, but Slocum couldn't read anything in them.

"It is," he said. "If you can't take our word—"

"Twenty-two hundred then or the full amount now," demanded the man with the silk cravat.

"Oh, it's only money," said Evangeline. "Don't argue so with them. I do want to get my ring back tomorrow, of course. Now will you escort me home?"

"Very well," Slocum said, aware that he was agreeing

to both the terms of the loan and to showing Evangeline home.

He held out his arm for her and together they left the Union Club. He was aware of the hard looks from the three men in the poker game, but that didn't bother Slocum as much as having to stick this lovely, generous woman with the full debt. She had guaranteed it, and she would have to pay it. There wasn't any way in hell Slocum could raise that kind of money in twenty-four hours.

2

Slocum felt an itching up and down his spine as he left the posh club. He kept thinking the three men inside who had taken him for twenty-seven hundred dollars would follow and demand their money now. He had no reason to believe they'd doubt they would get their money the next night. With Evangeline Dunbar's fabulous diamond ring as collateral, they had little to worry about.

Still, this was a considerable sum of money—and not just for John Slocum. The people scheming and gambling and living inside the Union Club had gotten there by never needlessly letting loose of a single coin. They might be terrible card players, but they were superb money handlers.

"I tried to warn you, sir," Evangeline said as they walked outside. A cool breeze whipped off San Francisco Bay and into Slocum's face. It dried the sweat that had been forming on his forehead. He was glad he hadn't had to shoot his way free. He knew he would have lost more than just a few dollars if he had tried.

"Seems as if everyone did," he said, remembering how the barkeep had hinted that Slocum ought to seek another game. "Do they work the club often?"

"I have no idea, sir. I have never seen them before in my life."

"The name's John Slocum. There's no need to call me sir. I don't rightly belong in such fast company."

"I recognized that right away. Is the suit rented?" Another woman might have turned this into a vicious question. Evangeline's voice carried the lilting, almost lyrical quality to it that made the query a shared joke.

Slocum looked down at the places where the suit bagged and the others where his tightly muscled body pressed hard against the seams. He had to laugh at himself. He wasn't cut out for this kind of a life. Or if he tried to live it, he ought to do more than rent it.

"A shop off Portsmouth Square rented it to me for the evening. Is it so apparent I'm not rich?"

"The rich are different," Evangeline said firmly. "There's an—odor to them that is indescribable. You feel it. It's more than power. I have known men with great power and little money. They don't have it."

"I think I understand," Slocum said. A railroad foreman had the power of life and death over his workers but he was hardly in the same class as Leland Stanford.

"You do not mind escorting me home, do you? I have had a bit of misfortune. My driver was taken ill, and I am not too good at handling a carriage."

"I am in your debt," Slocum said. He tried to do the honorable thing and tell Evangeline she was out twenty-two hundred dollars because he would never be able to repay her. Somehow the words jumbled in his throat. He decided he could see her home and perhaps find a better chance later. He owed her that much.

"Think nothing of it. I see you are a man of your word,

even if you don't have the kind of money it takes to frequent clubs like this.''

It surprised Slocum that she didn't press the point and ask how he had gained entry. She turned slightly and pointed to a small carriage, hardly the ornate variety Slocum would have thought fitting for a woman of her station.

He helped her up and climbed into the seat beside her. The nearness, the warmth, of the woman cut through the chilly San Francisco fog and made him feel almost happy. Almost. He hated to duck out on her, but he saw no other way. Slocum would see her home and then run like a scalded dog so that the card sharps could never find him.

"Drive down the hill and turn toward the bay," she directed. "It is so nice that you agreed to see me home. San Francisco can be a very dangerous place after dark for a woman alone."

"For anyone," he said, remembering how he had come by the membership card to the Union Club. He almost told Evangeline of his trials and how he had hoped to turn the five hundred dollars into a fortune, then bit it back. They rode in silence, Slocum stewing over his own greed.

He had been guilty of the very thing he sought in others. It had never occurred to him that the three players would be working together. He had played the same game with a friend on a trip along the Mississippi on a riverboat. By the time they had reached New Orleans, both had a fair grubstake.

"When are you riding on, Mr. Slocum?" she asked.

"What's that?" He hadn't been aware his thoughts were so transparent.

"I know you cannot possibly pay the amount you lost. The money you used to ante up was all you had, wasn't it?"

Slocum took a deep breath. There was nothing he could do but own up to his larcenous thoughts. "I am ashamed that I was going to leave you immediately after seeing you home safely. Your charity ought not be abused, but I have no choice.''

"Nonsense," Evangeline said. "I had a notion you couldn't pay. Those men will be happy enough with the ring—for a while. Only when you do not pay tomorrow night will there be grumblings and the beginning of real thought in their greedy skulls.''

"The ring is worth more than the gambling debt," he pointed out.

"Indeed," Evangeline said. Slocum wanted to press her on the point. Something about the offhand way she dismissed the ring's cost didn't set right with him. But he found himself knee-deep in trouble as suddenly as an ocean storm springs up.

"Stand and deliver!" cried a shadowy figure from the middle of the street. Slocum saw a long stave in the man's hand. Light from gas lamps turned the foggy scene into an eerie experience. Sounds were muffled and the world had collapsed into just a few feet along the street.

Slocum knew immediately that the man wouldn't be alone. Other footpads had to be behind Evangeline's carriage.

"John!" The brunette grabbed his upper arm and squeezed hard. "We can't be taken like this."

"Out of the way!" Slocum cried at the man in the street. He used the whip on the horse. The poor animal stumbled and then got its footing on the cobblestones. Slocum intended to run the man down. There was no reason to treat a highwayman with any consideration. If he stopped the carriage, the least the robber would do was steal everything Evangeline had of value.

Slocum didn't even want to think of what the worst might be. San Francisco was notorious for its crimps, shanghaiers who sold men to the clipper captains for impressed crew members. And Slocum was sure, if that was to be his fate, he would come out of the robbery much better than Evangeline Dunbar.

The Barbary Coast was filled with drugged whores who had been kidnapped. A woman as lovely as Evangeline would bring top dollar to the peddlers in human flesh. For a while.

The carriage leaped forward, then skewed to the side when it hit a large pole placed in the road. Slocum fought to retain control and failed. The carriage tipped precariously, teetered on one wheel for a moment and then toppled over. He was thrown out. Rolling, he fetched up hard against a building. Slocum shook his head to clear it. He saw the footpad advance on the carriage.

"John," moaned Evangeline. "Where are you?" He saw a delicate hand reaching out to find him. He wanted to go to her and tell her it was all right—but it wasn't. He had at least one robber to deal with.

The truth of the matter came to him when he heard the clicking of more boots on the cobblestones. At least two others joined the robber. As Slocum had guessed, they had positioned themselves behind the carriage to cut off any possible retreat.

His hand slid across his vest and found the pocket where the large caliber derringer rested. He had only two shots. He couldn't waste them. The small pistol slid free and came to his hand. He cocked the weapon and sighted carefully, centering on the first robber's body.

The explosion was damped by the fog, but the bullet found its indistinct target. The highwayman jerked around and then let out a shriek that would have drowned out anything less than cannon fire.

"'E bloody well shot me, 'e did!" the man cried.

Slocum readied the second barrel. He had hoped to make a clean kill. He still faced three men, one wounded and all the more dangerous for that. Slocum had seen a cornered, wounded rat rip the throat out of a healthy hunting dog. He wasn't about to let that happen.

"Where is 'e, mate?" came the question from down the

street. " 'E cain't 'arm a Sydney Duck and get away with it!''

Slocum cursed under his breath. He had run afoul of the most notorious of the Barbary Coast gangs. The toughest of them had come from Australian prisons and found the virtually lawless San Francisco to their liking. Slocum vowed not to fall prey to them.

"Over here," he said. The footsteps turned to pounding as the other two ran up. Slocum walked forward, arm straight and derringer ready.

"Watch 'im, 'e's got a gun!''

The warning did no good for the one in Slocum's sights. The bullet caught him in the center of his chest. He dropped to the ground as if his legs had turned to mush. Unfortunately, his friend's death did not even slow the other's mad rush. He came at Slocum swinging a long metal rod that swished as it cut through the air.

Slocum danced back and let the metal rod slash past him. Then he moved in, fists swinging hard. He felt as if he had tried to punch his way through an oak barrel. The footpad's belly was hard with muscle and Slocum's pounding had little effect.

"I got 'im. 'E won't escape me now!'' Strong arms circled Slocum in a bear hug. He gasped when the arms tightened, bending him backward. With his own hands trapped at his sides, he couldn't fight effectively.

The man's prodigious strength sapped Slocum of his. Slocum fought to keep from having his back broken. He kicked and tried to get his hands free. He couldn't. In desperation, Slocum smashed his head into the other man's face. Warm blood splattered over him. He had broken the man's nose.

The unexpected pain caused the man to let up on the horrible pressure circling Slocum. A quick twist got Slocum free of the punishing grip. He dropped to one knee and panted harshly as the other robber held his broken nose in disbelief.

Slocum rose and kicked as hard as he could. The man doubled over, no longer worrying about his broken nose. The Sydney Duck lay in the street, puking weakly.

"John, look out. Behind you!" came Evangeline's warning.

Slocum feinted to the left, turned, and went right. He spun to face the first robber. The man hadn't been able to swing his wood stave because of the wound in his shoulder. He wasn't as hindered using his knife, though. Slocum faced six inches of gleaming, deadly steel.

"Give it up," Slocum said. "Get your friends out of here and you might be around to rob someone else on another night."

The Sydney Duck paused, as if considering. Slocum saw the cagey look and knew the man was trying to set him up for the kill.

"Do you think so, mate?"

Even as he spoke, the robber launched an attack. Slocum dodged to the side, letting the man's knife hand slide past him harmlessly. Slocum caught the man's wrist in both of his hands and then twisted as hard as he could. Bones broke in the robber's wrist, and the knife clattered to the ground. Slocum didn't let up, however. He kept twisting until the man was flat on his back and staring up into Slocum's cold green eyes.

"Why shouldn't I kill you?" Slocum asked.

"Mate, it weren't nothin' personal. 'Tis just me job, it is."

Slocum drove his knee into the man's belly. Air gusted out of his lungs in a rush. It would be long minutes before he was able to do more than gasp for breath.

"Are you all right?" he asked Evangeline, helping her untangle her skirt from the wreckage of the carriage. She stood and brushed herself off. She looked past him to the three robbers. One was dead and the other two wished they were.

"You're more than I bargained for, John," she said in a small voice.

"Let's get you home."

"The carriage is a wreck."

"The horse is fine," he said. "Can you ride sidesaddle?"

Evangeline smiled and nodded. "I can ride any way I have to if it means getting out of here. This is not a nice part of town, is it?"

"Reckon not," Slocum said. He wanted to get as far away as possible before one of the men recovered enough to give their gang warning. A hundred Sydney Ducks might be after them if they stayed very much longer.

"My house is only a mile from here. Please, let's not tarry."

He helped her up onto the horse. She settled down and then motioned him to ride in front of her. Slocum climbed on, unaccustomed to riding bareback. He settled himself and got the feel of the animal under him. When Evangeline reached around his waist, he was ready to ride. His strong knees held firmly and guided the horse around. When he was sure he could control the carriage animal and that Evangeline wasn't likely to fall off, he put his heels to the horse's flanks. The horse trotted off briskly and soon brought them to Evangeline's house on Nob Hill.

Slocum let out a low whistle of appreciation. The house was a mansion.

"John," she said, slipping down from the horse without his aid, "please come in and check out the house. It has been such a—harrowing evening."

"What about your servants?"

"I—they've all been given the night off. They work so hard, I feel it is incumbent upon a good mistress to let them have some time to themselves."

"No servants?" Slocum jumped down and led the horse to the side of the house. He found a small stable and put the horse into a stall, fed the faithful animal, and decided he might curry it before leaving. It was the least he could do for Evangeline Dunbar.

"You're good with animals," she said. "You must spend a great deal of time out on the frontier."

"Spent some time there," he allowed. He was itching to return. The thought of the three men in the Union Club kept coming back to haunt him.

He turned and faced Evangeline. Her soft brown eyes looked at him with such trust he almost bolted like a spooked rabbit.

"This way," she said. "We can go in the rear entrance. No need to go around to the front."

He followed her, aware that his derringer was empty. He hadn't thought to bring extra rounds for it and his Colt Navy and other supplies were across town at a cheap hotel just off Market Street. If there was any problem in the rambling house, he'd have to take care of it just as he had back in the street.

Slocum sucked in a deep breath and winced. The Sydney Duck had damn near busted his ribs with his bear hug.

"I'll go in first," he said, when Evangeline reached the side entrance. He pushed past and saw that the door was already open. He stopped to examine the door but she crowded him and urged him inside.

"It's getting chilly out, John. The fog cuts right through to the bone. Don't you agree?"

He nodded and entered the house. He stood for a moment, every sense straining. He heard only the soft sounds of a house settling on its foundations. A deep sniff revealed a faint lavender scent, something he didn't quite associate with Evangeline. Still, he didn't catch fish or other harbor odors suggesting someone from the dock area had broken in. He went through the kitchen and into a hallway leading to the front room.

He paused at the stair landing and looked around. The dim light filtering in from a distant gas street lamp cast eerie shadows. He waited for something to move. The ghosts hiding in the dark were as still as Slocum was.

"It's all right, Evangeline," he said. "I don't think there's anything to worry yourself over."

"Thank you, John," she said, taking off her gloves and dropping them on a marble-topped table in the hallway. She paused and looked up the curving flight of mahogany stairs.

"What's wrong?"

"I—I don't know. Perhaps it's nothing. I am so on edge. I'm not used to being accosted as I was tonight."

Slocum listened hard but heard nothing from the second story. He said, "Let me go up first. I'll check it out."

She followed closely. He heard her soft breathing accelerate as they reached the top of the stairs.

"There," she said, pointing to the second door along the hallway. "In there."

He opened the door to a darkened room. Slocum stepped into the room and paused, waiting for someone to move. The slick sliding sounds came from behind him.

He looked over his shoulder and saw Evangeline wiggling like a snake to free herself from her fancy gown. She stood in the doorway clad only in a frilly camisole.

"Go on in, John," she said in a low, husky voice. "It's my bedroom. I want to be safe tonight. *All* night."

He didn't have a chance to answer her. Slocum felt her warm body pressed firmly against him, then his lips were occupied with hers. She kissed him hard. It took him a second to recover his composure. Then he returned the kiss with as much passion as it had been given. His lips parted slightly and let her tongue dance across the tip of his.

He felt himself growing stiffer. Then Slocum yelped. Evangeline had reached down and gripped the tight crotch of his fancy pants and lifted.

"To the bed, John. Unless you want to make love standing up."

"No, no need," he said, inching toward the four-poster bed. Evangeline pushed when he got close enough and he toppled backward onto the goose down quilt covering the bed.

"Do you like it?" she asked.

"I love it," he said, his eyes on her.

"No, silly. Not this." She pirouetted and somehow contrived to slip a little out of the camisole, letting the tops of her creamy breasts show. Evangeline wiggled and the silky garment dropped to her waist. Both breasts bobbed free and bounced. "Not these. That!"

She indicated the canopy of the bed. Slocum didn't want to take his eyes off the delectable sight before him, but he did. He almost laughed. Crowning the top of the bed was a huge mirror. Whoever was on the bottom could see in reflection everything that went on.

"We rich folks do know how to enjoy ourselves," she said. Evangeline jumped onto the bed and straddled Slocum's waist. She began picking at his fancy duds, then gave up. Fingers like claws tightened and ripped his clothing off.

"They're rented," he half-protested.

"You're not going to return them," Evangeline said, "any more than you were planning on repaying me."

"Listen, Evangeline—"

"Later," she said. "We can talk about it in the morning." She bent forward and silenced him with her kisses. She continued ripping and tearing at his clothes until he was naked on the bed under her.

Slocum decided he was letting her do too much of the work—or have too much of the fun. He reached up and cupped her breasts. Squeezing the lushness he found brought forth tiny squeals of joy from Evangeline's red, red lips. She tossed her head back like a frisky filly and settled down on top of him.

Her hips twitched and rotated slightly, then he found himself buried balls deep in tight female flesh. He gasped with the way she vibrated all around him. It was as if a velvet glove had taken firm hold of him and started squeezing rhythmically.

"I always wondered what it would be like to ride a bucking bronco," Evangeline said, looking down. He started to take his hands away from her breasts. She stopped him, holding his hands firmly in place. It was her turn to gasp with pleasure when he found the coppery nubs at the tips of those fleshy mounds. He squeezed on her nipples, teasing and stroking them until they were hard with arousal.

"Watch, John. Watch what's going on in the mirror," she urged. She bent forward, her naked hips beginning a back-and-forth motion. He felt himself leaving her moist, clinging interior. He wanted to stop the retreat. His hips lifted off the soft bed and tried to follow hers. He failed.

When only the purpled tip of his shaft remained within her pink nether lips, the motion reversed. Evangeline slammed down hard around him. Slocum watched the process in the mirror and felt the fires igniting in his loins. He wasn't sure if it came from watching the sexy woman's movements or the physical sensation of her all around him.

It didn't matter. He was groaning with delight now and had to have more.

Slocum sat up and sucked on one of her breasts. His tongue teased the nipple and then quickly moved to the other. Evangeline shook all over like a leaf in a high wind.

"I need you, John. Don't stop now. Do it to me. I need you to do it now!"

Slocum turned on the bed and got the woman onto her back. Her legs rose to either side of his waist. He looked down into her face, but she wasn't looking at him. Her gaze was fixed on the images moving so erotically in the mirror above. This was fine with Slocum. Let her enjoy the sight as he had done.

His hips moved faster. Every thrust got harder, more insistent. He felt the softness around him tensing. The friction mounted, and he was sure he was burning himself to a nubbin. He was past caring. Carried by the age-old rhythm, he let himself go.

Evangeline shuddered and let out a piercing shriek of joy

just as his seed spilled. Slocum kept moving, slower, with more deliberate movement, for another few minutes until he went entirely limp.

Finished, he rolled onto his side and held Evangeline Dunbar close. She burrowed her face into his shoulder and whispered, "We have much to talk about in the morning."

Slocum held her until her regular breathing signaled that she had gone to sleep. He would wait a while longer, then slip away. He didn't want to do it, but there wasn't any way in hell he could ever repay this generous woman. Saving her from the footpads might be repayment enough for the twenty-two hundred dollars she would be out, but he didn't think so. Not after tonight.

3

Slocum awoke just as the sunlight crept through the lace curtains dangling across the east window. It took him several seconds to remember that he wasn't in a cheap hotel down on Portsmouth Square. He turned and looked at the woman sleeping peacefully beside him.

Evangeline looked like an angel in the morning light. Her soft brown hair drifted in a cloud across the white linen, framing her perfect face and bringing a catch to Slocum's throat. It wasn't easy making love to her, then leaving.

It was even harder leaving her with his gambling debt, but he wasn't under any illusions about being able to pay. And men like the three who had bamboozled him weren't likely to accept his promise to pay later. They had Evangeline's diamond ring; that was likely all they were ever going to get. For that, Slocum was sorry. He owed the woman and he'd repay her. Someday, somehow, he'd repay her. But it would have to be in the future. He intended to get the hell out of San Francisco while the getting was good.

Slocum slipped soundlessly from the bed. The cool sheets moved across his naked body and caused him to remember what had happened to his fancy rented cutaway. The tattered garment lay on the floor where Evangeline had discarded it. She had finished the job of ripping it up started by the three Sydney Ducks. Slocum lifted the rags and knew he couldn't wear them. There just wasn't enough left to cover any part of him decently.

He looked around and saw Evangeline Dunbar sitting up in the bed, her doe-like brown eyes fixed on him.

"I told you it was all right, John. You need not creep around like a sneak thief."

"Evangeline—"

"Forget the money you owe those thugs. They cheated you. They don't deserve it."

"You left your ring with them. I don't want—" Slocum was getting confused. He didn't think well with his pants off like this, and something about the way the woman acted didn't set right.

"The ring's not important. It was only a trinket."

"Trinket?" Slocum was astounded. The ring must have been worth far more than the twenty-two hundred dollars he had lost and Evangeline tossed off its loss as if it were nothing.

"You feel guilty about taking money from me, don't you?" Her brown eyes sharpened and Slocum felt as if he were now the hunted and no longer the hunter. "You don't even like the idea of running out and sticking me with your gambling debt."

Slocum only nodded. He looked around to find something to wrap around him. Evangeline wasn't going to let him get away this easily. As she sat up in the huge four-poster bed, her naked breasts were caught by a bar of honey sunlight coming through the window. Slocum found it harder and harder to think straight with all the distractions. What bothered him the most was that Evangeline knew his problem and played on it.

"Do you want to earn the money, John? I have a—chore that must be done soon. Today, if possible."

"I don't kill for money. I swear, you'll get your money back. I don't steal money from women."

"I know you're not a hired killer. You're a hard man, but you don't have the look in your eye. And no cold-blooded murderer would worry about duping a poor little ol' thang out of a few paltry dollars." Evangeline mocked him with the put-on Southern accent.

"What am I supposed to do for the money, if not kill someone?"

"I assure you, it's nothing illegal. There might be some shooting, but it would be to protect me. I need a traveling companion and guide if I am ever to see my brother again."

"Your brother?" Slocum was kept off-balance by the rapid turns in the woman's logic. She had gone from accusing him of stealing her money to telling him he could earn it and now she was mentioning a brother. "Where's your brother?"

"That's the problem," Evangeline Dunbar said. "He's in Utah. At Fort Desolation."

Slocum just stared at her. Borneo was hardly farther away than Fort Desolation.

Slocum stood at the edge of the platform and looked down the tracks for the train. It was fifteen minutes late. He didn't want to believe this was a bad omen, but something gnawed away at his guts and told him it was. Letting Evangeline Dunbar talk him into escorting her to Desolation Point, Utah, was about the dumbest thing he had done since getting into a game with three men in cahoots.

"I'd go right away by myself," he heard her saying. Slocum hadn't been paying much attention. He was still edgy about skipping out on the gambling debt. The ring was nice but the gamblers would want gold for Slocum's loss. There was no reason to think they were coming after him, but that didn't stop him from looking guiltily over his shoulder every few minutes.

He wished to hell the train would arrive.

"Yes, I'd be off like a shot," Evangeline went on, not noticing that Slocum wasn't listening. "My father's death took me by surprise. He was a hale and hearty old gent." She dabbed at a tear in the corner of her eye. "He just upped and died one day."

"When?" Slocum asked, more of the nonexistent train than the woman.

"About a week ago. The inheritance is considerable." She looked squarely at him and said, "You saw the house. That is only a portion of it. I *must* reach my brother and tell him of our dear papa's death."

"If he's a cavalry officer as you say, there's got to be a telegraph line nearby. Never knew a horse soldier that could be out of touch with his superiors without getting downright antsy," Slocum said.

"There is no need to use the telegraph. I know my brother is present at Fort Desolation," Evangeline said, "but I need his signature. There is no other way to get it by the deadline."

"What deadline?" Slocum gave up waiting for the train and sat beside the lovely woman.

"I thought I'd mentioned it. Neither William nor I get a red cent unless he signs the proper papers by the end of this month." Evangeline patted a small case she carried, indicating that the legal documents were inside.

"That's a mighty peculiar will," Slocum said. "I've heard of women not collecting anything, but never has a man ignored both son and daughter without good reason."

"The law is complicated, John," Evangeline said primly. "I do hate dragging you off like this, but it is important. William shall be very, very rich when he signs the documents." She smiled wickedly. "And so shall I."

"How do you plan to spend your riches?" Slocum asked.

Evangeline's hand wandered over and rested on his thigh. "I haven't given it much thought, but I'm sure I'll think of something. I might need help, you know."

Slocum started to check their luggage—Evangeline's luggage. All he had was a bedroll with his spare Colt Navy and a decent saddle. The rest of the small mountain of suitcases and trunks was hers. She held him back for a moment.

"Don't rush off, John. There's no reason to be frightened of me, even if I have seen you with your pants off."

He started to protest, but she bent forward and kissed him. She smiled wickedly. "There. Go off and do whatever you intended. And do see if you can't hurry the train. It was supposed to be here twenty minutes ago."

Slocum checked the gold watch in his vest pocket and saw she was right. The train was twenty minutes late, and his brother Robert's watch did not lie. He stared at the open case and remembered his brother with fondness. A tall, handsome man, he had fought valiantly during the war. But the ill-considered Pickett's Charge had taken his life after almost two years in combat without so much as a scratch. The softly ticking timepiece was all Slocum had to remind him of better days back in Calhoun, Georgia.

The rumble and hiss of a steam engine caught his attention. He looked down the tracks and saw huge plumes of black smoke. The train was finally pulling around the long, gentle curve and into the Oakland station. Slocum didn't look forward to the train trip. He preferred a good horse under him to the mechanical snorting and chugging of a railroad train, but traveling with so much luggage was easier by train.

He would never have any good memories of the ferry from San Francisco to the Oakland station. He had almost gotten seasick during the short half hour trip, and Evangeline had insisted on him personally seeing to each and every one of her bags and trunks. Slocum felt obligated to the woman but being her servant wasn't to his liking.

The train would get them to Desolation Point, Utah, far faster than on horseback. The sooner he found her brother and left Evangeline in his care the sooner Slocum could get about his own business.

Still, the trip looked to have its benefits. Evangeline Dunbar was one gorgeous woman, and he had already found out that she was extraordinarily talented in many ways. Any man could count himself as lucky spending time with her.

Slocum motioned to a porter to help load the luggage. He spoke briefly with the conductor about going straight through to Cedar City in southwestern Utah.

"You got to be kidding, mister," the conductor said, shaking his head emphatically. "There's *nothing* in that part of the world, leastwise as far as railroads are concerned. Might be a year 'fore the tracks get laid through those mountains. You can get a ticket to Elko and then see about headin' south from there."

"What else is around Cedar City?" Slocum asked.

The conductor shrugged. "Saint George is close by, but there's no tracks going in there, either. Friend, that's desolate territory. The best you can hope for is to hop off the train near the Utah–Nevada border, get horses, and go south that way."

Slocum looked at the mountain of baggage. It would take a full-scale pack train of a half dozen mules to get all Evangeline's belongings to Fort Desolation.

"Yep, there's nothing worth mentioning in that part of the world. You thinkin' on gettin' on aboard now? Train's pullin' out in five minutes—on the dot."

"Hope you're keeping more to the schedule getting to Utah than pulling in to Oakland," Slocum said.

"We had a spot of trouble with a loose rail, mister. Nothing to worry about. Get aboard."

The conductor made a last minute check, circling the train with the oiler and his long-spouted oil can. Only when he was sure everything was as it ought to be did he climb into the first passenger car, lean out, and bellow, "All aboard! All aboard!"

Slocum stood on the rickety platform for a moment, lost in thought. There was no decision to be made about accompanying Evangeline to Desolation Point, Utah. He had already cast his lot with her; he owed her this much—and more. This was another worry that nagged at him. Something just didn't seem right. He looked around, up and down the platform for the other passengers. From the corner of his eye he caught sight of a thin, angular man dressed in a long black coat swinging into the last passenger car. He tried to remember if he had seen the man earlier. He couldn't. He had been too upset over the delay to pay proper attention to the other passengers clustered at the far end of the train station.

The engine belched white steam and followed that with clouds of black soot. The mighty wheels began turning. The smell of hot steel and the grinding of powerful pistons assaulted his senses. Slocum grabbed a convenient handle, jumped onto the train, and swung into the passenger car. He walked slowly, studying the people in the seats. A few of the men wore sidearms, too, but none had the dangerous look of a killer about him. These were law-abiding men who wore their six-shooters to make sure everyone they met stayed law-abiding.

These men Slocum could accept. They posed no danger to him or Evangeline. As he walked, he fumed. What was the burr under his saddle? He was jumpy for no good reason.

He almost laughed as he left the passenger car and went into the next one where Evangeline waited for him. There was plenty of reason. He was playing nursemaid to a beautiful, rich woman—or a woman who would be rich if he got her to Fort Desolation. A more out of the way place might exist on the planet, but John Slocum couldn't think of where it might be. The trip was hazardous by its very nature, but not enough to make him this uneasy. He couldn't shake the feeling of someone walking on his grave.

"John, there you are. Come and sit down. I wondered where you'd gotten off to." Evangeline patted the seat beside her. He settled down on the hard seat, making sure his Colt Navy rested easy in its cross-draw holster.

"Just seeing to the bags. There's something of a problem about those bags, Evangeline," he said. He explained that the rail line did not cut south from the Salt Lake City–Oakland route.

"Elko?" she said. "There's a city named Elko?"

"It's in Nevada, less than a hundred miles from the Utah border," he told her. "That might be our best bet for finding horses and riding south to Desolation Point."

"If this is the only way to get to my brother—" she said, her voice trailing off.

"It looks to be our best chance," said Slocum. He didn't know if he wanted to tackle this subject yet. He took a deep breath and launched into it. "But there's a problem with your baggage. There's too much to take on the trail."

"I shall consider the dilemma," Evangeline said. She stared at the countryside slipping by outside the window. The woman hugged the case with the legal papers she needed her brother to sign and said nothing more. Slocum leaned back in the seat and tipped his hat down over his eyes. While she thought, he could sleep. He didn't doubt there would be many sleepless nights ahead.

Slocum awoke with a start, his hand reaching for his six-shooter. It took him several seconds to remember he was on a train. It took his sleepy brain several more seconds to realize that Evangeline was missing.

For a few minutes he didn't worry unduly about it. She might be relieving herself in the small room at the side of the car. When a tall, bulky man emerged from the tiny room, Slocum knew that Evangeline was gone. He pushed himself to his feet and looked around. A small boy sat a few seats away, staring at him with big eyes.

"Son, have you seen the woman traveling with me?" Slocum asked.

The boy nodded.

"Where did she go?"

The boy pointed toward the rear of the train.

"How long ago did she leave?" Slocum was tiring of being the only one talking.

"She and the other men left 'bout ten minutes ago."

"Other men?" Slocum went cold inside.

"Three of them. One wore a long black coat, sorta like the undertaker who buried my father."

Slocum didn't ask anything more of the boy. He had obviously seen enough trouble in his short life. Slocum didn't want him seeing more. As he pushed through the connecting doors between the cars, he checked his Colt Navy. It was ready for action.

He got to the baggage car without finding Evangeline or the men. He paused before he entered the heavily loaded car. If they weren't here, they had to be in the caboose. Slocum opened the weighty door a crack and peered inside. The darkness was relieved by a flickering oil lamp at the far end.

Not sure if this was a clerk or the men he sought, Slocum advanced cautiously. He wormed through a pile of bags, then edged around, his six-shooter going in front of him. One man had Evangeline pinned against the wall. The other two stood nearby and leered. It was everything Slocum could do to keep from gunning the trio down. As far as he could tell, they hadn't done anything more than scare her a mite, but from their expressions they wanted to do a world more.

"—tell us," the one holding Evangeline demanded. "If you don't, we're gonna heave you outta the train." He motioned. One man worked to slide back the baggage car's side door.

Slocum hadn't realized he had been asleep so long. Black forms flashed by the train. It must be well nigh midnight. They had passed through the Coast Range and were moving quickly through the dry central valley of California.

"We won't just *toss* you out," the man promised. "We'll

drag you along. That purty face of yours will get all cut up. Nobody'll recognize you. Nobody.''

"Don't," Evangeline pleaded. "I can't help you. I— oh!" She pretended to faint, then tried to squirm free when the man's hold relaxed. The ploy didn't work.

He slammed her roughly against the wall. "I'm losin' my patience. Do I let Len and Gutherie here bounce you along the cinders for a mile or two or do you want to talk to me?"

"No!"

He grabbed her and shoved her toward the one Slocum had pegged as being Gutherie. Slocum left his hiding place and walked forward, not hurrying, not dawdling. He reached the man's side just as Gutherie saw him. The man never had a chance to avoid the blued steel barrel of Slocum's pistol. Metal crunching into bone sounded louder than the train's clacking steel wheels. Gutherie tumbled out into the night without making a sound.

Slocum spun, his six-shooter leveled. The one he had decided was Len was already reaching for his hogleg. Slocum fired, then stepped to one side as Len danced past into the night.

"John!" shrieked Evangeline. "Look out!"

He didn't need the warning. He knew the element of surprise was long past. The man who had held Evangeline was going for his own six-gun. Slocum never gave him the chance to draw. The two men were too close for either to get off a good shot.

Slocum recognized it first and acted. His arms circled Evangeline's attacker in a bear hug. He grunted as he lifted the man off his feet and swung him around. Then Slocum simply let go. The man sailed off into the night, just as he had promised to do to Evangeline.

Slocum faced the woman. Evangeline stood with her brown eyes wide in wonder. For an instant Slocum saw more than fear there. He saw cunning. Then she masked it and threw herself into his arms to sob against his shoulder.

Slocum wondered just what the hell he had gotten himself into this time.

4

"Who the hell were they?" Slocum asked, staring into the darkness rushing by the train. It had been several minutes since he had tossed the last of the kidnappers out the baggage car door. By now they were all a mile or more behind the train. From what he could see of the countryside, it would take them some time before they could get to a town and find horses, if they survived the fall to the ground.

"I do declare, John," Evangeline Dunbar said, straightening her mussed brown hair, "I have never put up with such rudeness. The quality of traveler these days is ever so low."

"Rudeness, hell!" flared Slocum. "They wanted to kidnap you." He tried to simmer down. He had overheard enough of the dialogue between the kidnappers and Evangeline to know they weren't simply out to rob her—or worse. They had wanted information, and she had refused them.

"Perhaps that's so," she said. She batted her long eyelashes at him. When she saw it wasn't having any effect, she changed tactics. "They must have known I would be rich after William signs the papers. They must have wanted money."

"They didn't say?"

She paused as if to consider all he might have heard. She shook her head when he kept a poker face.

"You're lying," he said. "You know why they tried to kidnap you. Why? What did they want?"

"I'm telling you, John. They wanted money. I—I think I'd seen their leader back in San Francisco. He must have been hanging around the Union Club. Talk there is loose when it comes to one's station in life. My father's inheritance had to be the topic on more than one set of lips. Those people are all like that."

"Those people? Your kind of people?"

Slocum took a moment's pleasure in seeing he had momentarily unsettled Evangeline's usual calm. Whatever she said now might be the truth, the truth shaken free from the concrete bonds of her other lies. He didn't know what was going on but he wanted to find out. Not only Evangeline's but his own life might depend on it.

"I'm not a member of the Union Club," she said.

"Do you know Leland Stanford?"

"Of course I do. He's a good friend of the family. My father had railroad business with him often. Nothing gets done in northern California without Leland's approval. He is *very* powerful. You might say he *is* California."

"I know that. What I don't know is why those men grabbed you on the train. Who were they going to collect their ransom money from?"

"Why—" She hesitated. Then Evangeline said, "They might not have thought this through. They might not have known my brother needs to sign the papers for any of us to get our inheritance. Nothing says road agents are smart."

"They weren't road agents," Slocum said. He didn't know exactly what they were, but they had the look of gunfighters about them. They were bully boys sent to do another's bidding. But they weren't after any money Evangeline might carry with her. Not once had they even bothered to pick up her purse and rummage through it. Slocum bent and tossed the small purse to the woman.

His thoughts were obvious. Evangeline quickly opened the purse and found her wallet. She let out a tiny sigh of feigned relief. "Thank goodness, they didn't take my money."

"They weren't after your money. They weren't out to ransom you, either," he said. "What did they want?"

The coldness in his green eyes convinced her he was not going to be put off this time with extraneous rambling.

"Very well, John. I owe you a great deal for saving my life—twice. They were going to kill me if I did not cooperate. Did you hear that much?"

She was still probing to find what he knew and didn't know. Slocum felt an obligation to her for what she had done to erase his gambling debt. He had forgotten the cardinal rule of gambling and had gotten greedy. Evangeline had bailed him out of a dangerous situation when he needed it most. Her owed her for that. But the question rising in his mind was simple: How much did he owe her? He had rescued her twice. How many more times equalled twenty-two hundred dollars?

"Tell me all about it," he said, wondering what sort of story he would get. He had a gut feeling it wasn't likely to be the truth—or at least not much of it.

"My papa was rich and powerful. He moved in high circles."

"What was his business?" Slocum cut in.

"He did a little of this and a lot of that. He was very successful at it." Evangeline cleared her throat and gave him the look a schoolmarm might give a misbehaving student. She went on. "It is impossible for a man as powerful as my papa not to accumulate enemies. He drew them like flies." She smiled at this little witticism.

Slocum was listening closely. Everything he heard sounded fine so far. Evangeline's house on Nob Hill had been more of a mansion than anything else. She was obviously known at the Union Club, even if she wasn't a member. What the woman might have meant was that her father had belonged to this select group and that she merely accompanied him on occasion. It wasn't likely, after all, that a woman would be admitted to such a posh club as a member.

"He had a business partner," Evangeline said. "Papa and he did not get along well toward the end. I think those men worked for him."

"What's it to him if you're on a train going to see your brother?"

"Really, John, do I have to spell everything out for you?" She stamped a petite foot and looked disgusted. "If I cannot get William to sign the papers, we do not inherit my father's half of the business. That means his business partner gets it all. It is certainly to his benefit to stop me from reaching Fort Desolation."

"Why didn't you tell me this before?"

"Men," she said in dismay. "You can be so dense at times. Would you have wanted to accompany me if I'd told you the trip might be dangerous? I think not."

Slocum shook his head. This didn't ring true. He had known it was going to be a long and perilous journey. Anytime you went into Indian country, anytime you rode to a place called Desolation Point, it wasn't going to be a Sunday social.

"I'm obligated to you. Of course I'd've still escorted you to the fort," he said.

"Really. John, I'm touched by your honor. Most men aren't like this. Forgive me. I misjudged you terribly. I don't know how I can ever get you to forgive me."

Evangeline's words were apologetic but her slightly parted red lips were demanding. She caught him up in her arms and caused him to stagger back a few paces until they tumbled together onto a large pile of canvas sacks on the floor. They made love in the baggage car, supported by a dozen mail bags, and Slocum never noticed how lumpy this new mattress was.

"If they have a lick of sense," Slocum said, "they'd hightail it to a town and get on the telegraph." He was studying a map of the railroad trying to figure out where it was most likely they would run into more henchmen sent by Evangeline's father's business partner.

"Elko is a major intersection of railroads," she said. "A spur runs south and the main line goes on to Salt Lake City."

"It's not a major junction," Slocum corrected. "There's no track going south. None at all."

"But the map—"

"It's wrong," he said. "I asked about travel from Elko to Saint George or Cedar City on the train and got laughed at. There might be some track getting laid from Salt Lake to Cedar City, but no one seems to know for certain. This here map was put out by the railroad showing where they'd like to run line someday. There's no telling if it will ever get laid. We're going to have to make our way south some other way."

"Oh, my," she said, genuinely startled at the revelation. "I had counted on being able to go the entire way on a train."

"There might be another way," Slocum said.

"Horses?"

He nodded. Slocum preferred being out on the range, even if much of the way south would be through the Nevada desert. He didn't know how well Evangeline would stand up to the hardship. It was early spring and the intense heat had yet to burn its way into the alkaline soil, but the nights were freezing and the trip wouldn't be pleasant.

"I can ride," she said. "Remember the night of your

gambling spree at the club? I rode behind you back to the house.''

"That was different," Slocum said. "And there's no way we'll be able to take all your gear. Something will have to be left behind." He tried to soften the blow for her. *Most* of what she had brought along would have to be left. Unless they hired out a dozen pack mules, they'd never be able to wrangle the trunks and suitcases stacked head high in the baggage car.

"I can make do with less," Evangeline said dubiously. "When do you think we'll reach Elko?"

"The train's supposed to arrive day after tomorrow."

"You make it sound as if we're not going to be on the train when it does."

"We won't," Slocum said. "If those men want you bad enough, they've already telegraphed ahead. There'll be an army waiting for us—if we stay with the train."

"We can't just leap off here." Evangeline looked into the night. Tendrils of dawn poked pinkly at the eastern sky. The empty land stretched into the twilight in any direction she cared to look. It was a desolate land but one Slocum preferred to company like the ones who had jumped Evangeline.

"There's a whistle stop coming up in about an hour. I talked with the conductor, and he says they have to stop to take on water."

"In this country, I can understand that." She turned and her brown eyes went wide with disbelief. "You can't possibly suggest we cut across Nevada and head down to the corner of Utah. Why, it will add days and days to our trip!"

"I reckon it might cost us a week or more." He had decided it would be closer to two weeks, and this was only if they made good time without experiencing any delays. The Indians weren't active. Leastwise, Slocum hadn't heard of any raids in this part of the country. Down near William Dunbar's section of Utah, it was another matter. Raiding parties kept the horse soldiers at Fort Desolation busy.

That was a hurdle Slocum would cross when they came to it.

"This is so unexpected. The hardship. I am unused to such travel," she said.

Slocum waited for the woman to come to a decision. He half expected her to back out and tell him she wanted to return to San Francisco. She was a hothouse flower, and this was a dangerous trip. With the addition of the men following her, it made the journey to southwestern Utah almost desperate.

Evangeline surprised him. "This is of no real concern, however, John. We shall do it."

"Just like that? Are you sure you know what you're doing?"

"Of course I do. The papers must be signed. There is no other way for William and me to inherit. The time constraints are important, of course, but I believe I could get a judge to stretch the matter a mite, if necessary. But we dare not take more than a week or two longer than we had originally planned."

"I'll try to see to it," Slocum said, still shocked at her decision. The inheritance meant more to her than he had thought. Evangeline could marry well. She was a gorgeous woman who traveled in San Francisco's better social circles. A good marriage would entitle her to wealth far beyond anything she might inherit from her father. Her brother was sure to get the lion's share of any estate.

"Very well. I need to sleep. Wake me just before we get to the next station."

"I will," Slocum said, turning back to the inaccurate railroad map. He pored over it, estimating distances and the difficulty of travel across barren terrain. It wasn't going to be as bad as he had thought, not for a few days. If they managed to avoid the men pursuing Evangeline, all the better.

When the train began to slow, Slocum gently shook

Evangeline. Her eyes snapped open. A small smile crept across her lips. "So soon?" she asked.

"I'm afraid so." Slocum leaned out the window and tried to get some idea of the town's size. It didn't look good to him, but this was the only other stop before Elko. If they wanted a good enough head start, they had to leave now.

"Go on back to the baggage car and pick out one case," he told her.

"One?"

"That's all you're going to be able to take. If you have any trail clothes, be sure to put those on. We'll be passing through some rough country over the next week or so."

"Of course."

Her easy acceptance again took Slocum by surprise. Evangeline Dunbar was a continual source of contradictions. She was from a privileged class and yet managed to cope well with his demands. Another woman would have argued. Getting to her brother had to be a powerful goad.

Slocum dropped from the train to the ground and walked to the water tower. It took him only a few seconds to find the source of information he knew would be lurking there. Two young boys watched eagerly as the engineer and the oiler worked to swing the huge spout in position over the top of the engine.

"Either of you know where a man might purchase a few horses?" Slocum asked.

"Reckon so," said the older of the two boys. "My pa runs the livery in town."

"Yeah, and he's also the only vet in purty near fifty miles," said the other.

"Reckon he knows good horseflesh then," said Slocum. "I'll give you each a nickel if you help the lady and me with our gear." He pointed toward the baggage door. Evangeline was struggling to push open the heavy door. A single valise sat on the edge. She had changed into clothing adequate for the trip.

When Slocum and the two eager boys went back to get

his saddle and Evangeline's bag, he was startled to see how well worn the woman's clothing was. This wasn't an outfit she had picked up at a fancy ass clothier because she thought it was chic.

"Why are you staring?" she asked. "Don't you like it?"

"Can't find any fault with it," Slocum said. "You fill out them britches a sight better'n anyone I ever saw."

"I'll take that as a compliment. Who are your two young friends?"

"Their pa runs the livery. We'll be needing to buy horses and I reckon this is as good a place as any." Slocum pointed to his saddle, bedroll, and saddlebags. The older boy wrestled them to the ground and then hefted them. The younger one took Evangeline's bag and stared in open admiration at her.

Slocum let the boys lead the way. He had to have a few words with the woman in private.

"I'm going to need about a hundred dollars for the horses," he said.

"Isn't that a bit much for two horses?" she asked.

"Four horses. I want to be able to trade off every hour or two so's not to tire any single animal overmuch. We can make half again the distance riding that way."

"But if you only purchased two horses, the cost wouldn't be over fifty dollars," she said.

"True. So? And I'll need another ten dollars for supplies. A canvas desert bag would be a good buy, and we need enough food for a week or longer. I don't want to stop and hunt game along the way. Until we hit the mountains, there's not likely to be much more than a few rabbits and a rattler or two to eat."

"John," she said. Evangeline chewed nervously on her lower lip.

"What's wrong?"

"I've only got fifty dollars total. The rest went to buy the railroad tickets."

"But—" He stared at her. She was rich. She had to have more than fifty dollars with her.

"That's all I've got. Take it, but there won't be any more."

Slocum took the wad of greenbacks, mostly rumpled ones and fives. He made do because he had to. An hour later, they rode out of the small town with a minimum of supplies and only two horses. It was going to be a more difficult trip than Slocum had anticipated—or wanted.

5

They had been traveling through the desert for six days, angling through Nevada toward the southwestern corner of Utah and Desolation Point. During their entire trip Slocum hadn't seen another living soul. It was as if God had reached down and plucked all other humans from the face of the world.

Fort Desolation. The name rang in Slocum's head like a cracked bell. He didn't like the sound of it. The emptiness was wearing on him and a sense of impending danger grew with every step his pony took. Nothing was working out the way he had thought when he'd agreed to escort Evangeline to meet her brother at the army post.

The horse he rode was a valiant pony, but hardly strong enough to keep up the pace he wanted. Evangeline's mare was little better, but they were the best he could do for twenty dollars apiece. The woman's lack of money still bothered him, and it had been almost a week since they'd left the whistle stop.

At first he had come right out and demanded to know why she didn't have more money. She had spoken for more than twenty minutes. He had grown tired of listening to her explanation—especially since there wasn't any logic to it. She rambled and made circular arguments and always got back to saying she had left San Francisco thinking they wouldn't need much.

That wasn't like anyone with money Slocum had ever known. Leland Stanford might travel without so much as a wallet, but he was surrounded by men who carried hundreds of dollars for any emergency. Slocum had to think that Evangeline Dunbar simply didn't have the kind of money she pretended.

Slocum rode a bit behind the woman, staring at her. She was an enigma to him. She'd be rich, she said, if her brother signed the documents she carried. But she lived as if she were rich back in San Francisco. Riffraff simply didn't get into the Union Club. This thought made Slocum smile wryly. He had gotten in where he didn't belong, but that had been a special case. Taking his former employer's membership card was something that wouldn't happen often.

But Evangeline? Slocum just didn't know. She acted as if she had all the money in the world. She saw nothing wrong in giving the three gamblers an expensive diamond ring worth far more than the money owed and then not bothering to ransom it back. When it came down to actual cash, though, she just didn't have it.

"John," she called back, "can we rest a spell? I'm getting mighty tired. And my horse is starting to wobble again."

"We'll get off and walk them for a while," he said. He dismounted and went to help Evangeline down. He need not have bothered. She had already slipped from the saddle and stood rubbing her rump.

She saw his attention and smiled wickedly. "Would you like to do this for me?"

"Later," he said. This was something else he didn't quite understand. Their relationship was more than hired help and mistress, but it was also less than lovers. He enjoyed sleeping with her, but at times he felt as if she were a thousand miles away. Evangeline showed passion and expertise, but there was an emotional layer through which he had never penetrated. He wondered if anyone had ever reached the real Evangeline hiding inside. Somehow he doubted it.

She was tightly wrapped up in herself and only came out of the cocoon when it suited her purposes.

He settled down to walking, reins dangling loosely from his left hand. He picked his way through the lumps of alkali, only occasionally lifting his face to the purple mountains in the distance. Fort Desolation lay beyond that range. Another two days' travel would see them safely at the army post.

What then? Slocum wasn't sure he had a good answer for that. Evangeline would get her brother's signature and they would be rich. No doubt they would return to San Francisco to face their father's former business partner and claim their rightful part of the company.

Slocum frowned. He couldn't remember if Evangeline had said what business her father had been in. The more he tried to put together the pieces of the woman's life, the less he found. For all the time they had spent together, both in bed and out, Evangeline was particularly tight-lipped about herself.

"John," she said quietly. "Do you see it? There, in the distance, up high."

He saw it. The column of white smoke shifted with wind currents blowing down the mountain slopes, but the individual puffs were not natural. Indians were signaling. Who? About what? From all he had heard, there wasn't much Indian activity now, except for the rumors of the Cheyenne leaving their Oklahoma reservations.

"There, see that, too? What's going on, John?" The

woman pointed a bit to the south of the smoke signals. A mirror flashed repeatedly.

"Indians signaling back and forth. One side used a fire and smoke signals. The other's got a mirror."

"What are they saying?"

"Heaven alone knows," Slocum said, trudging on toward the mountains. He had a feeling gnawing at his guts that they would find out before they reached the safety of William Dunbar's fort.

Three days after they had first seen the smoke signals, they reached the foothills. Slocum thought he knew the way through the mountains over to Desolation Point, Utah. But he was tuckered out and his horse wasn't in any condition for the steep passes and rocky trails.

"We can't just stay here, John. I need to reach William *soon*. Time is running out."

"We can't push the animals any more. Hell, I'm not sure we can push ourselves much more. It would have been better if we'd been able to buy spare mounts and maybe brought along some grain to feed them. We could have made it here a couple days earlier."

He lay back, head resting on his bedroll, and staring up into the azure sky. Thin white clouds like cracked fish bones moved in echelon formations across his field of vision. He was drifting off to sleep, a warm breeze coming off the desert and mingling with the juniper-scented air from the hills.

He came awake with a start. It took him a second to realize he hadn't been fully asleep. He had reached for his Colt Navy and had pulled it halfway from its holster.

"What's wrong, John?" Evangeline stared at him in surprise, her brown eyes wide and guileless.

"I don't know. Something's been eating at me for a couple days."

"The Indians?"

"Maybe," he said. The Indians weren't going to go out

of their way to ambush a man and a woman traveling across the desert. Once in the mountain passes, it was a different story. That was not white man's land. And he had heard accounts of other Indians moving through the area. There might be a range war going on between the tribes.

"I'll scout ahead a ways. Don't go riding off without me," he said.

"Silly. I know better than that. I'd get lost within a mile." Evangeline stared into the mountains and shivered. "I just want this to be over. I hope William's at the fort when we get there."

"Any reason he won't be?"

"You know how it is with soldiers. All the time out on patrol. William wrote me once saying he was gone from Fort Desolation more than he was there. If there are Indians lurking about, he might be chasing them back to their reservations or whatever he has to do."

Slocum nodded as he saddled his complaining pony. A cavalry officer wasn't worth his salt unless he was out doing something. A garrison soldier was the worst there was. They fell back onto strict observance of regulations and made life hell for their men. The best officers kept their troops alert by patrolling.

With the Indians around, an officer might keep his men alert and dying on patrol. Slocum had to get some idea of the danger they faced before going farther.

He kissed Evangeline and then rode slowly along the trail, keen green eyes alert for any sign of recent passage. Four miles along the trail he found the first spoor. It might have been nothing. Then he found a beaded medicine pouch with a cut rawhide string. A careless brave had lost his amulets and fetishes.

Slocum poked at it, examining the beadwork. He took a deep breath and let it out slowly. This was northern Cheyenne. They must have left their Oklahoma reservation again in an attempt to return to their ancestral grounds along the Tongue River in Montana. Why they had come this way

Slocum couldn't hazard a guess. But they had. No other Indian would carry such potent medicine from another tribe.

"Cheyenne," he muttered as he looked around. Cheyenne. That made for one savage war party ready to lift any white man's scalp coming through what they considered their territory. But something still didn't seem right to him. He was missing a small detail.

Slocum mounted and started back down the trail to where he and Evangeline had camped. On impulse, he took a branching canyon, intending to come out some miles to the north of their camp and then follow the same trail they had used earlier in the day. He wanted to see if anyone tracked them. There wasn't any good reason for his suspicions, but Slocum always listened when this sixth sense told him of something wrong. It had kept him alive through the war and ever since.

The ride was as lonely as it had been across the Nevada desert. He made his way down the canyon and came back into the foothills, some ten miles from where his camp was. Slocum had ridden only a few hundred feet when he saw bright, shiny scratch marks on the rock.

Dismounting, he studied the deep cuts in the rock. The scoring had been done recently and by a shod horse. Slocum knew his or Evangeline's horse might have been responsible, but he doubted it. The entire area was covered with evidence of horses. When he found three fresh piles of horse manure, he knew someone had been close on their heels.

He swung back into the saddle and checked his six-shooter, loading the one empty cylinder he usually rested the hammer on for safety when he rode. Satisfied that it was ready for action, he drew the Winchester from its saddle scabbard and loaded it completely. He was ready for bear. Human bear.

Slocum tried to figure out how many men he tracked. They were white men. He knew that for certain; beyond riding shod horses, he saw evidence where they had stopped for a spell and one man had spit tobacco juice repeatedly at a small tree. His aim had been damned good. The tobacco juice was already killing the low-growing juniper. The longer he rode, the more cautious Slocum grew.

The men he trailed were in no particular hurry. So they wouldn't be seen, they stopped and rested, waiting for their quarry to go on. Slocum got a cold lump in his belly when it came to him who the band was probably following.

Throwing caution to the winds, he urged his tired horse forward. The pony let out an annoyed whinny, then gave the best effort remaining in its tired legs. Slocum looked around constantly, anticipating an ambush. When he didn't run into armed men, his gut churned even more and he tried to get more speed from the horse.

The additional prompting caused his pony to dig in both front legs and try to throw him.

"There, there," he said, trying to soothe the animal. "We've got to get back to camp pronto. Evangeline's got a world of trouble coming down around her ears, unless I miss my guess."

The horse wasn't mollified. Slocum had to let the pony pick its way through the rocks on the trail and couldn't change the slow pace. By the time he got to the top of a rise and could look down to where he and Evangeline had camped hours before, he knew what he would see.

Their small campfire smoldered, a thin column of white smoke twisting its way upward. His bedroll was to one side, laid out neatly as only Evangeline could do it. Her own gear was safely stashed beside his. But of the woman and her horse there was no sign.

Slocum dismounted and grabbed his rifle. He left the horse to graze while he investigated. The closer he got to camp, the less vigilance he showed. The area was empty. The only living thing he scared off was a jackrabbit timidly poking its long-eared head from a burrow.

"Damnation," he said, kicking at his bedroll. Slocum took a deep breath and tried to calm down. Evangeline might have taken it into her head to just ride off somewhere and look at the sunset—but he didn't think so.

Dropping to the ground and looking carefully at the dirt, he figured out all that had happened.

Three men had ridden into camp. Another two had circled and come up from behind. He figured the three had kept Evangeline busy and let the other two do the dirty work. Evangeline must have fought. He found pieces of her clothing and a bloody patch in the dirt where someone had bled a considerable amount. He even found a hunting knife that had been dropped in the scuffle.

Slocum poked at the knife. It had a carved elk horn handle and was made of good steel. It hefted wrong, though. He looked it over and decided the handle had been drilled and filled with lead. This made it a vicious weapon in a fight. The point would come up easily, and the weight in the user's grip added to the power of a cut or stab. The carving on the handle made it difficult for the knife to slip free. No one carried such a knife and then casually forgot it.

The knife had been dropped as Evangeline Dunbar fought to keep from being kidnapped.

But who? What white man would go to so much trouble to track her down, wait for Slocum to leave, and then rush in to take her? There was too much the woman hadn't told Slocum.

He hunkered down by the still-warm fire and stared into the dying embers. He had to make a decision and make it quick. Should he go after her or just butt out of what was obviously a more complicated fight than Evangeline had revealed?

6

Slocum tried to figure out where the riders might have gone and how far ahead of him they would be. If they had put Evangeline on her horse, the distance between the camp and wherever they were now couldn't be too great, Slocum knew. Her horse had been tiring even faster than his own. If the men had ridden into the camp immediately after Slocum left this afternoon, they wouldn't have more than four hours' head start. It was a considerable amount but not insurmountable if Slocum kept his head—and Evangeline did the same.

If she did what she could to slow the men, he had a chance against them.

Slocum felt his stomach growl and knew he couldn't go on right away. He dug through his provender and came up with a can of beans and a can of peaches. He had been saving the fruit for later in the trip. He thought he needed it now. The beans were heated in the fire's embers while he wolfed down the peaches. By the time he had finished, the beans were warm enough to stomach.

He finished with a long draught from the desert bag, still hanging from a nearby bush. Slocum slung his equipment over his shoulder, took the canvas bag, and trudged back up the hill to where his horse contentedly cropped at the sparse grass. The pony looked at him out of one huge brown eye and seemed to shudder. The horse knew what was expected of it and didn't like the idea one whit.

"Sorry about this," Slocum said, meaning it. He hadn't figured out how much of everything Evangeline had told him was a lie, but some of it had to be. Who were the kidnappers? It hardly seemed likely her pa's business partner would come all this way after her.

Or would he? Slocum reckoned the man could fight his cause better in a courtroom with a bought judge and jury. Sending men to kidnap her was reckless and might come back against him in the long run. Still, there were the three men aboard the train—and maybe five more in the small band that had been trailing them for a day or more.

Slocum wished he knew more about Evangeline's father and about his business partner. For that matter, he wondered about their corporation. What were they involved in?

He snorted, tiny plumes of condensation rushing into the cool night air. For that matter, what was *he* involved in?

"Evangeline," he muttered as he rode back down the hill and through the camp. He left what belongings had been discarded earlier. They would only weigh him down. Right now he needed the sturdy pony to keep moving, no matter what. It was going to be a long, hard night for both man and mount.

Just a little after dawn and almost falling from the saddle with sleep, Slocum jerked around and heard two men arguing. He blinked and rubbed his eyes. He hadn't even been sure he was following the right trail most of the night. The canyon had branched several times and the last fork hadn't given him a clue as to the kidnappers' direction. He had simply guessed, working on instinct more than actual knowledge.

Instinct had paid off once more.

Slocum stretched and patted the exhausted horse's neck. Now that he had found the men—he hoped they were the kidnappers he pursued—he had another problem facing him. Simply riding up and taking Evangeline back wasn't the answer to his problem.

They outnumbered him five to one. Their horses were reasonably fresh and even if he sneaked into their camp and spirited Evangeline off, they could run him down by noon, no matter how fast he ran.

Slocum tethered his horse some distance away and pulled out his Winchester. He didn't cotton much to the notion of gunning the men down in cold blood, but he wasn't in any condition to get the woman back in any other way. Slipping closer and closer to the camp, he dropped to his belly and wiggled like a silent snake to within fifteen feet of their campfire.

The aroma of freshly brewed coffee made his mouth water. All he had drunk during the night had come from the smelly desert bag. Slocum almost passed out from the sight and odor of the bacon sizzling in a cast iron skillet and the bread one man sat and ate. Each huge chunk of the bread going into the man's mouth made Slocum just that much hungrier. He had eaten, and was glad for it, but his stomach still rubbed against his backbone. He was going to have to make quick work of the men or he would do something foolish just to get their food.

Slocum rolled onto his back and came to a sitting position. He began a slow survey behind him. He still wasn't sure how many men were in the party that had kidnaped Evangeline. The last thing he wanted was one of the men sneaking up on him from behind.

Sure that the way behind was clear, Slocum began a circuit of the camp, studying every rock for shelter, every depression for a place to ambush them. They had chosen well enough, either by design or luck. He wasn't going to be able to tackle five men without getting himself into hot water.

"Got to get on back," he heard one man call out. "You boys take it easy on her. Don't so much as touch her now, you hear?"

Slocum scampered forward and dived into a gully to get a better look at what was happening in the camp. Two men had mounted and were talking with the remaining three.

"He's not gonna mind if we just sorta entertain her, is he?" asked one of the men remaining behind.

"He'll have your liver for breakfast if you try. You know how the boss is about her. You understand?"

"Sure, sure," said the one who had been making lewd suggestions about what they might do with Evangeline. "She's as safe as if she was in some angel's hip pocket."

"You'll be buzzard bait if she ain't," promised the other. He wheeled his horse about and started off a brisk trot. The other mounted man hurried to follow. The three left in camp watched them go. Only when the pair was out of sight did anyone speak. It was the cowboy who had suggested all the things he wanted to do to Evangeline.

"Evans is getting purty big for his britches. What call's he got tellin' us what we can and can't do?"

"The boss—" started another.

The third man cut in. "Evans is only speaking the truth. You know how riled the boss gets when things don't go his way."

The first man spat and scratched himself. "That's the truth. Look at how he dragged us all the way out here to this god-forsaken country just for the likes of *her*." He pointed toward a bedroll. Slocum saw movement and knew where Evangeline had been put for safekeeping.

"She's not got enough meat on her bones for my taste," said the third. "Let's play some poker."

"Skinny or not, I'd rather have her than lose more money

to you in any damn card game.'' The first man hitched up his trousers and moved toward the bedroll. Slocum heard tiny trapped animal sounds from under the blanket. When the man pulled back the blanket Slocum saw that Evangeline had been bound and gagged. She was trying to scream but only muffled grunts came out.

"Look at her. Ain't she a sight for sore eyes? I been waitin' for a woman like you all my life.'' He started unbuttoning his trousers.

Slocum pulled his Winchester out and drew back the hammer. He sighted carefully.

"Don't go messin' with her, Luke. You heard Evans.''

"To hell with Evans. I'm gonna enjoy this one. If you two owlhoots keep your tater traps shut, nobody's gonna know. I might even share with you—later on.''

He kicked the blanket aside and dropped between Evangeline's legs.

It was the last thing he ever did. Slocum's bullet entered his left armpit, dug through heart and lungs, and exited on the other side of the man's body.

The other two stood and stared dumbly. Then they both shouted incoherently and dived for cover. Slocum got off a second shot but missed.

He knew better than to stay in the gully. He had to get around the pair and make them think they were surrounded by a dozen men. If he didn't and they got the idea into their heads that he was alone, they could flank him and put an end to the gunfight. Slocum rolled and came to a kneeling position. He saw the battered rim of a Stetson rise incautiously from behind a half-buried boulder. He put a bullet through the dusty hat.

"There's two of them,'' came the cry from behind the rock where the hat had so rashly appeared. Slocum decided it had been a ruse to draw his fire. That was all right. He wanted them to think they were up against overwhelming odds. He fired again, then started running, trying to get into position to take out the second man.

He saw Evangeline struggling to sit up. The man he had gunned down lay across her legs, pinning her to the ground. Slocum wanted to call out and warn her to stay low but didn't dare risk it. The smallest lapse of attention would mean both their deaths.

And the pair that had ridden off might hear the gunfire and return to investigate. If they did, Slocum wanted the odds cut down to his favor.

"There's three of 'em," said one man. "I heard one up there on the hillside. Don't let 'em get the high ground, Joe. Don't! They'll cut us down for sure."

Slocum didn't know what the man had heard. Probably nothing more than a rabbit running for its burrow. Whatever it was, it provided a much needed diversion. Slocum pulled back on the rifle's trigger just as the man reared up to get a better view of the hill. The bullet caught him squarely in the chest. He sagged back, dead, without uttering so much as a sound.

Two down and one to go. Slocum kept moving, hurrying around the second corpse.

"Joe? What's wrong? Where did you get off to?"

"Here," Slocum said in a low voice, hoping the other man wouldn't notice the difference between him and his friend. It didn't work.

"Son of a bitch!" the man cried. A hail of bullets chipped away at rock all around Slocum. "You killed Joe! I'm gonna flay you alive for that. He was my best friend. You stinkin' son of a bitch!"

Slocum kept his calm as he continued to move. Let the remaining man rant all he wanted. The angrier—the more frightened—he got, the easier it would be to take him. Slocum moved to a spot where he had a good field of fire through the camp, but he arrived just seconds too late. The last gunman had reached Evangeline's side and held his six-shooter to the side of her head.

"Give up or the bitch dies. You got ten seconds. Do it now, damn you. Do it!"

"John, please," moaned Evangeline. She had succeeded in getting the gag from her mouth and one hand was free, but with the pistol at her head she was still a prisoner—and one to be used against Slocum.

"Yeah, John," shouted the gunman. "Get your ass out here. You and the others, too. I want to see you all or I put a bullet through her damned head."

"Let's talk this over," Slocum said. He slipped the thong off the hammer of his Colt Navy, then laid down his rifle. He stepped out into plain sight, hands at his side. "You kill her and you're dead meat. There's no reason to keep you alive if she's dead."

"I want out of here," the man said. His voice cracked with strain. Slocum knew he was spooked and wouldn't react rationally. "I don't care if the bitch dies."

Slocum took a step forward, then motioned as if shooing his posse away. Only then did he say, "You don't have a snowball's chance in hell. Give her over to us and then you can ride on out. We don't have any quarrel with you. It's with your boss." Slocum was bluffing. He didn't have any idea who the man worked for. All he could do was rely on the snippets of conversation he had overheard as the other two men had ridden away earlier.

"You're a liar. You'd never let me go."

"Let her go. I'm giving you my word." Slocum's hand was moving even as the words left his lips.

His hand flashed to the ebony handle of his six-shooter. He drew and cocked the pistol in a smooth action and fired. The bullet caught the gunman squarely in the shoulder, spinning him around. Slocum stepped to one side, cocked, and fired a second time. This bullet smashed the man's spine. He lay twitching on the ground like a stepped-on snake.

"John!" Evangeline Dunbar was horrified at what he had done. "He could have killed me!"

"He'd've killed the both of us," Slocum said. "I knew there wouldn't be any way to talk him out of it, so I shot him.'' He stared at the twitching body, wondering if he ought to use a third bullet. Before he could decide, the man's twitches faded and he lay still, facedown in the dirt.

"He could have *killed* me!"

"Given half a chance, he would have," Slocum agreed. "It was a risk but it worked out."

"I could have died!"

He wished she would quit harping on it. He had seen that it wasn't possible to simply sit back and gun the kidnapper down. Evangeline was too good a shield for that. Slocum had bluffed his way closer and then relied on his skill to remove the obstacle to their freedom. Evangeline might have been hurt because of his tactics, but she would have definitely been killed any other way.

"We're both alive and all three of those bastards are dead," Slocum said coldly. "Now let's get the hell out of here before the other two return. They must have heard the gunfire."

"I could have been killed," Evangeline muttered over and over, but she did as Slocum told her.

The one good thing about the kidnapping, as far as Slocum could see it, was that they now had spare horses. There wasn't any reason to let the three animals tethered near the camp go to waste. And unless he missed his guess, they'd need to travel far and fast if they wanted to stay ahead of the men on Evangeline's trail.

7

"How many of them are there?" asked Slocum. He craned his neck to get a better view of the terrain in front of them. In the darkness it was hopeless. He might be riding into a Cheyenne war party and never know it until it was too late. Or he might be following the same trail taken by the two men who had ridden from the camp where Evangeline had been held. There might be a dozen road agents lurking ahead.

He turned and looked at the woman in the dim starlight. She rode stiffly, her head fixed like it was set in concrete. Evangeline looked neither left nor right and she did little to give him any hope that he'd find out what the hell caused this mess.

The more Slocum thought on it, the less he understood. The men on the train had been after Evangeline for some reason. Angry business partners didn't traipse halfway across the West to kidnap the daughter of a rival. Even if

Evangeline getting her brother's signature would ruin her father's business partner, the courts were more amenable to persuasion. A few dollars could buy any judge and jury in San Francisco. Why send a small army after her?

"Who were they?" Slocum asked.

She muttered something he didn't quite catch. He repeated the question. The brunette turned and glared at him.

"Don't ask so many questions. Just get me to Fort Desolation. I need to talk to my brother right away. This is serious, John. You can never know how serious it is."

"I know," Slocum said angrily. "I almost got my damn-fool head blown off finding out." He tried to calm down and put his thoughts in proper order. "Back on the train. Those kidnappers were part of this same band, weren't they? And you know who they work for."

"Of course I do. Quentin isn't going to roll over and play dead just because we're almost done. He was my father's rival in the shipping business. I told you all about it."

Slocum filed away the notion that Evangeline's father was in the shipping trade. That was something she hadn't told him before. Truth to tell, there wasn't much she had told him.

"How many men are after you?"

"What? Only Quentin, but that's enough. He's ruthless. He won't stop until he's got me."

She turned back to stare directly ahead. He wanted to see what messages flashed across those brown eyes of hers. She was mad but there was an element of desperation to her gestures that hadn't been present before. Slocum didn't think it had anything to do with her close brush with the three back at the camp, either. Evangeline Dunbar didn't scare easily.

They rode in silence for several miles, the trail rising steeply and the rocky path vanishing entirely. Slocum let his tired horse pick its way through the mountainous terrain until it started to stumble repeatedly. He got off and changed to one of the captured horses to give his a rest. Evangeline's horse was doing better so he said nothing to her.

The wind whistling through the gap in the mountains was the only sound carried on the night air other than the clicking of their shod horses' hooves against the rock. Slocum used the silence to think hard. He didn't know how much more he owed Evangeline. He couldn't simply abandon her, but he needed to know more. It didn't take a genius to figure out she wasn't telling him a fraction of what she knew— and what he needed to know to keep them both alive.

Quentin, whoever he was, had sent men on their trail. Back on the railroad car had been a mere hint of the men following them. Slocum had seen another five and the two leaving had sounded as if they were reporting to a larger group.

"Ten?" he asked aloud. "Are there at least ten others on your trail?"

"Quentin never travels alone," Evangeline said, distracted from her own thoughts. "He's got this thing about being alone. Can't stand it. I think he needs someone to order around."

"Are there more?"

"More than ten men with him? I doubt it. He always was something of a skinflint. That's the way bankers are, you know. Tighter than a pair of mail order shoes."

Slocum started to ask if Quentin was a shipping magnate or a banker, then bit it back. Evangeline was lying to him. He had caught her in a moment when she wasn't thinking of all the other lies she had spun together out of whole cloth.

This ended any sense of responsibility toward her. She had rescued Slocum from a tight fix back at the Union Club, but the price of a diamond ring didn't give her the right to put his neck in a noose without knowing all the details of her problem. For all he knew, Quentin was a lawman on her trail. Slocum doubted that from the way the men in his posse worked, but their behavior meant little. Because he hadn't seen any deputies' stars didn't mean they weren't sworn in and duly authorized to arrest her.

He shook his head. He was working with smoke and shadows. The men on the train hadn't wanted to arrest Evangeline; they had wanted information she wouldn't give them. The ones he'd just left back in the camp weren't acting as if they had arrested a felon, either. It was more like a hunter bringing down a ten point buck. Evangeline was a prize to be captured rather than a reward to be collected.

The wind died down and was replaced by the whistle of his breath in and out of his lungs. The higher they got in the mountains, the more Slocum struggled to keep moving. He was hungry and hadn't rested in more days than he could remember. The trek across the desert had been wearing. The arduous trip up the mountain pass was rapidly draining what little reserves he had.

"We've got to camp for a while," he told Evangeline. "I can't go on much longer. Neither can the horses."

"We can switch off. That's what you said we should have done before." She hadn't noticed he had already done so. She was as lost in her own thoughts as he was in his.

The money—or Evangeline's lack of it—was another point that dug at Slocum's mind like a nettle caught under the skin. She was rich and had all the trappings but—

He wasn't sure what to make of the lack of servants at the woman's house, the absence of a carriage driver the night she had bailed him out at the Union Club, or the paltry number of greenbacks she had brought along on the trip. She had to know they would need money during the trip to Fort Desolation—and she definitely knew that Slocum didn't have any.

Too many questions and no answers. Slocum looked over at the woman trying to find a spot free of rocks to sit down. He wouldn't be getting the truth from her. She kept too much to herself.

"I don't think they'll be able to pick up our trail in these rocks until morning," Slocum said. "That'll give us a good start on them. By then we can be rested and ready."

"I'm thirsty," Evangeline said. "Where's the canteen?"

Slocum sloshed the desert bag and found very little water. This didn't please him. In the mountains there were always springs and pools fed by runoff. They weren't high enough yet to find snow. That was both a blessing and a problem.

He'd trade a cold night for a mouthful of pure water, because he hadn't seen any springs on their way up into the low mountain pass. It had been a dry year.

"Don't take too much," he cautioned, passing Evangeline the canvas bag. "We'll need it later."

"What of the horses?"

He shrugged. They'd have to fend for themselves. The few clumps of new grass might give them a drop or two of moisture, but it surely wouldn't give the animals much in the way of a good meal.

"We're in a tight spot," he admitted. "We'll need some luck to get out of it."

"We're not that far from the fort," Evangeline said. "My map shows it only twenty or thirty miles off."

"What map is that?" asked Slocum. He glanced over at his saddlebags where his own map still rode. He saw a corner poking out from under the leather flap.

"I've got one of my own," Evangeline said. "One my brother sent. It's not as good as yours."

Slocum settled back and unrolled his blanket, rearranging the rocks under it the best he could. A few poked into his back, but he had slept on more uncomfortable beds in his day. When Evangeline snuggled up close, her blanket over them, the rocks seemed to fade away.

"We'll make it, won't we, John?" she asked in a soft voice. "You'll get me to the fort?"

"I'm trying."

"It might not be easy. Quentin never gives up. That's what makes him so dangerous. He and my papa worked twenty hour days getting their mercantile open."

"Mercantile?" he asked, frowning.

"They ran a store. Dry goods, things like that. It blos-

somed after they got it running. There are a dozen stores
spread through the Bay Area now. Fabulously profitable.
You know how much everything costs in San Francisco. It
has to be brought in from Boston, around the Cape, or
overland on the railroads. My papa got the idea of shipping
goods in from the Orient, but there wasn't too much people
wanted from the Celestials other than their laundry done
right.''

''So your father and this Quentin were partners in a
store?''

''Not just any store, John. It was *big* and Quentin's trying
to take it from my brother and me.''

Shipping, banking, dry goods—what was her father's
business? Why did she continue to lie to him? He had proven
to her that he wasn't going to abandon her. The continual
lies could only poison anything more between them.

Slocum lay with his arm around Evangeline's shoulders.
In a few minutes her soft, warm breath caressed his chest.
She had slipped into a deep, untroubled sleep. Slocum lay
on his back and stared at the hard diamond points of the
stars.

Just what had he gotten himself into? The stars were just
like Evangeline. They didn't give him any good answers.

They rode into the rising sun. Slocum squinted and tried
to keep his eyes on the valley floor where the trail ended.
He was growing increasingly uneasy and couldn't pinpoint
the reason. Evangeline hadn't spoken a dozen words to him
since waking almost an hour earlier. That was fine with
him. His mouth had turned to cotton. Hers probably wasn't
much better, due to the lack of water. The valley promised
some moisture and forage for the horses.

But the sense of danger mounted with every step toward
the valley.

''There,'' Evangeline said. ''There's some water. I'm
ready for it. I can hardly spit, my mouth is so dry.''

''Take the rest of the water,'' Slocum said, passing over

the desert bag. There was hardly enough for a good mouthful. He had been saving it in case they hadn't found water soon.

The horses began straining, wanting to rush down to the small creek meandering along the valley floor. Slocum reined in and just sat, watching. His spirits sank when a bright flash from the far side of the canyon was answered by another below them.

"Did you see that?" he asked Evangeline. "Mirror signals. There are Indians down there."

"So? We can negotiate with them. They wouldn't stop us from drinking the water. It's not theirs, after all. This whole land is claimed by the government. At least, that's what William says. His post has to patrol all this land."

"They might be Cheyenne off the Oklahoma reservation," Slocum told her. "They're just passing through to their ancestral lands up in Montana. If that's so, they'd as soon scalp us as let us drink. We're the enemy."

"We haven't done anything to them," she said, a touch of uneasiness in her voice. She was trying to make it sound better than it was. Slocum knew the woman understood the danger. Thirst was making her invent reasons to go straight down to the stream.

"It's your brother's job to send them back to where they escaped from," Slocum pointed out. "They won't take kindly to anyone who might report their whereabouts to the cavalry."

"My papa was the best lawyer in San Francisco. He never gave up just because it looked hopeless. I'm not about to give up just because some savages stand between me and my brother."

Slocum squinted into the sun and tried to keep his peace. Her father was a lawyer now. Banker, merchant, shipping magnate, who knew what the man might become if the trip lasted long enough and Evangeline got tired and thirsty enough.

"We don't have much choice," he said, looking back

over his shoulder. He tried to guess how fast Quentin and his men might have been able to trail them. Even if the pursuing man had taken his time, he would be able to close the gap because Slocum and Evangeline were so tired and thirsty. They hadn't traveled well. Returning to the mountain pass was out of the question. Better to take their chances with the band of Indians passing through the valley.

"We might be able to keep out of their way," Slocum said, thinking out loud. "I can't tell if the signaling was warning about us or if it had to do with something else."

"I need water," she said. "I'm giddy and I can barely stay on my horse." Evangeline swayed to emphasize her point. Slocum decided she wasn't playacting much at all. He was having trouble keeping his vision from turning blurry.

"Let's go," he said, coming to a decision. If they had to fight, let it be at the stream. The gurgling water drew him powerfully. The Cheyenne might ambush them, but at least Slocum would die with a bellyful of water.

They angled back and forth down the side of the mountain until they reached a green patch near a small grove of cottonwoods. Slocum knew this was the most likely spot for the Indians to have camped. He wanted to warn Evangeline back, to give him a chance to scout and see what danger lay ahead.

She put her heels to the willing horse's flanks and raced past. Slocum sighed and drew his rifle, waiting for a target to pop up. When Evangeline vanished into the stand of trees and he heard no twang of bowstring or slash of knife, he followed her. When he reached the woman, she was drinking deeply from the shallow creek. Her horse was slurping water noisily and would bloat quickly.

Slocum pulled the horse back and let the others drink. Only when they were finished did he quench his own thirst. The water slipped down his throat, sweeter than any wine, headier than any whiskey. He wiped his mouth on his sleeve and rocked back on his heels and looked around for any sign of Indians. There was only the tranquility of a mountain stream and the small animals that lived off it.

He stared at the woman still drinking from the clear creek. Evangeline was oblivious to his scrutiny. She led a charmed life. She had been at the right spot back in San Francisco to get him to escort her to Fort Desolation. She had eluded Quentin's men twice and now they seemed to be free to drink the water. Where the Indians were who had done the signaling, Slocum couldn't say.

It was even possible they could make it on into Fort Desolation without any problem. He doubted if they were two hours' ride away. Evangeline Dunbar led a charmed life. Slocum just hoped some of that luck would rub off on him before she got him killed.

8

"I feel much better," Evangeline Dunbar said. She sat beside the stream, her face and hands clean once more and another long drink swallowed from the creek. She had filled the desert bag and was ready to push on.

Slocum wasn't quite ready yet to start for the fort. He had given the horses another chance to bloat themselves from drinking too much, then pulled them back when he saw their bellies starting to expand. Their raucous neighs of protest worried him. It might be better to let the animals kill themselves than bring the Cheyenne down on their necks.

He shook his head. He wasn't even sure if the Indians he had seen signaling to one another were Cheyenne. They might be Ute or Crow or who knows what. It hardly mattered, though. Any Indian party was not likely to take kindly to white men disturbing them. The cavalry had not treated any of them too fairly.

"I'm going off for a few minutes," he told her. "Stay in camp and watch the horses. If there's any trouble, ride like the wind for the fort. Don't stop for anything."

"What are you going to do, John?"

"Scout around, like I ought to have done before we came down to the creek."

"Why bother? There aren't any Indians here. They would have attacked us if there had been, wouldn't they?"

"Probably. I just want to be sure we don't blunder into a war party by accident. Better to sit tight and let them pass by than to go tearing straight into them."

"I reckon that is so," Evangeline said thoughtfully. "We aren't far from the fort, are we?"

"You're the one with the map," he said almost nastily. She hadn't mentioned she had a map of the area until it had just come out. The map he had was out of date and not much use—and she had never looked at her map in his presence. Evangeline was hiding something, but he couldn't tell what.

He checked his Colt Navy, then started into the grove of cottonwoods. In a few minutes he blended into the dense undergrowth tangling their trunks. Slocum fell to the ground and wormed his way around like a snake. He circled and came back to spy on Evangeline. Slocum wasn't sure what he was waiting for her to do. He had left, only to return and watch her. If there were any Cheyenne nearby, they would hear him long before he found their camp. He was good, but they were on the run from the cavalry and wouldn't be careless. A single mistake would mean they would be returned to the hated reservations in Oklahoma.

He lay flat on the ground under a thorny blackberry bush and just waited. He had no idea what to expect from Evangeline. Whatever he had expected to happen, it didn't. She sat and simply waited patiently, hands folded in her lap. Fifteen minutes of observation convinced Slocum he wasn't going to learn anything. He slipped away, cursing the spots where the thorns tore at his shirt and the flesh under it. If there had been ripe berries, his situation would have been more fortunate. However, it was too early in the season for more than a few buds to have formed.

But the thorns! They had cut his arms and back and left shallow, bloody grooves.

Slocum returned and motioned for Evangeline to mount up.

"No luck?" she asked, seeing the cuts and tiny trickles of blood.

"Nothing," he said. He dabbed away some of the blood with a rag dipped in the stream and then climbed onto his pony. The animal was more rested and content now that water and some grass had been provided. "How far to the fort?"

"Twenty miles," Evangeline said. "Maybe not that far."

"I want to be inside by nightfall," Slocum told her. "There are too many people out after our scalps for my liking."

"Having walls and a cavalry troop to protect you can be a comfort," Evangeline said. Slocum looked at her sharply, not sure if she was ridiculing him.

They rode until late afternoon when Slocum raised his hand and motioned for the woman to stop. She reined in beside him.

"What's wrong?" she asked. "That's the road into the fort. See how well traveled it is? The cavalry must use it to come and go on patrol. We're almost there."

"I know," Slocum said. "There's a problem, though. We're not the only ones on this road."

"A patrol?"

Slocum slipped from the saddle and looked briefly at the marks in the dirt. He said, "Indians. The horses aren't shod. And they came by here within the past hour. See how distinct the tracks are? Any wind would have rounded the edges."

"They were here sooner than that, John," Evangeline said softly.

"How can you tell?"

He looked up and saw the reason for the woman's statement. A line of a half dozen Cheyenne braves rounded a curve in the road not a half mile away. The sunlight caught on their shiny ornaments and the steel tips of their lances. This wasn't just a band of Indians passing through. It was a war party.

"They haven't seen us. They're heading toward the fort," Slocum said in a low voice. He wasn't sure if his words would carry on the wind to the Indians but he wasn't taking any chances. The six braves were more than a match for him and Evangeline. All he had was his rifle and side arm. Evangeline had a derringer hidden away that he had given her, but their weapons would mean nothing in the face of the Cheyenne warriors.

"Do we just stand here in the road or do we hide?"

"Hiding isn't going to be possible," Slocum said, looking back over his shoulder.

"And why not?"

He pointed. Just as she had spotted the braves in front of them, he had seen the ones behind. Another group of three rode quickly along the road—and they had seen the two travelers. Whoops of glee sounded like a death peal in Slocum's ears.

"Let's pretend we can escape them," Slocum said. "Does that map of your brother's show any way to Fort Desolation other than along this road?" The road wound back and forth as it followed the twists and turns of the canyon.

"I didn't look," Evangeline said. She started to pull the map from her bodice where she had hidden it.

"Do it from memory. We've got to ride." Slocum saw a low pass that seemed like a plausible spot for another trail into the cavalry post. It was off the main road but showed signs of being traveled recently. He put his heels into his pony's sides. The horse seemed to understand the urgency, either from his tone or from the war cries from the Cheyenne. It exploded like a lightning bolt for the break in the rocks.

If nothing else, Slocum thought as he bent low over the horse's neck, they could reach the high ground and kill one or two of the warriors. He didn't have any hope of killing all three Cheyenne braves. Even if he took one by stealth, the other two would let out a ruckus loud enough to call half the nation down on their necks.

"I can't ride much more, John," panted Evangeline. "This is wearing me out. I do declare, it doesn't seem as if I've rested in the last two weeks."

"You won't be worrying about resting any more if we don't get away from them." He jerked his thumb back down the hill in the direction of the pursuing warriors.

They got to the pass and Slocum got a chance to see what lay ahead. It didn't look good, but there might be some small glint of hope. Below, almost two miles distant, lay Fort Desolation. He couldn't keep pushing his horse, even downhill, and hope to beat the Cheyenne there. He had to try something.

"Keep going," he ordered Evangeline. "I'll stay and hold them off."

"No! We are in this together. We can fight them off together or die trying."

He admired her spunk if not her good sense. He might be able to force the braves to cover and use the added time to catch up with her. The only way they were going to survive was to get to the safety of the fort and its troop of cavalry.

"Do as I tell you," he snapped. "I'll be along. You just watch out for the other braves who've taken the road. This looks to be a shortcut to the fort. You might end up there about the same time they arrive."

"They wouldn't be going to the fort. You said that the cavalry wanted them back in Oklahoma. Why should they tempt fate by riding on up to the main gate and announcing their presence?"

Slocum didn't have time to tell her about the Indians' skewed version of bravery. The Sioux carried feathered lances they used to touch their enemy—counting coup. It was a mark of distinction to escape to brag about it. The Cheyenne didn't count coup, but they had the same streak of crazy in them. Slocum thought it quite possible that the warriors would ride up and dare the horse soldiers in the fort to come and get them. It might even be a setup for an ambush.

The more cavalry the Indians killed, the fewer round eyes there were to come after them on their way north to the Tongue River.

Slocum pulled out his rifle and dropped to the top of a rock and waited. The braves came whooping and hollering up the hill behind. He sighted carefully and squeezed off a round. He cursed when he missed. The Indian moved at the last possible instant and saved himself a slug through the chest.

"John—"

"Go to the fort!" he shouted. "I'll keep them at bay as long as I can, then follow you down. Get help, damn it. Find your brother and get a few of those soldiers off their butts!"

He didn't turn to see if Evangeline obeyed him. He was too busy trying to sight in on a good target. The Cheyenne were too wily for that. They popped up, screamed, and then ducked back before he could get a good shot off. They moved well up the hill, distracting him on the left while the braves on the right flank moved forward. Slocum had to do something fast or they would be on top of him.

Slocum rolled to his back and came to his feet. Running hard to his left, he hoped to be able to flank the Cheyenne as they made their way up the hill. The narrow, rocky pass cut off lateral movement, but Slocum wasn't looking to make this a pitched battle. He just wanted to slow them down a mite.

He dropped back to his belly and waited. The chance

came. The braves didn't think he would abandon his position as he had—and certainly not to move to one side. If anything, they expected him to turn tail and run as Evangeline was doing. If he had done that, he'd have been buzzard bait within seconds.

One brave poked his head up just enough to look around. This would have been safe if Slocum had remained where he had started firing on them. To the Indian's surprise, he lost a piece of eagle feather to a well-aimed bullet. He jerked around in shock and caught a second bullet in the arm. Howling like a banshee, he dived for cover.

The sound attracted the second Cheyenne. He came over to see what had happened to his comrade. Slocum got another round into this warrior, causing him to limp slightly.

He knew there wasn't any way he could push the fight further. Two of them were injured, but not seriously. The third could bide his time and let the two wounded braves draw Slocum's fire. But the game wasn't going to be played that way. Slocum turned and raced for his horse. The pony shifted nervously, moving from one side to the other like a captive elephant Slocum had seen in a traveling circus. He vaulted into the saddle and urged the horse to its best speed.

Downhill, this wasn't too fast, but it took the Cheyenne by surprise again. They had left their mounts some distance down the hill to attack on foot.

Ahead, Slocum saw Evangeline riding steadily for the main gates of Fort Desolation with the captured horses racing behind her. The fort didn't look like much. The trees cut for its walls weren't very thick and its upkeep had been neglected, but he couldn't remember a sweeter sight in a long, long time. The promise of fifty cavalry rifles to push back the Cheyenne war party was downright reassuring.

Slocum let his horse have its head as the pony picked its way down the steep hill. He swung around and levered another round into the Winchester's chamber. He got off a couple sloppy shots just as the three Cheyenne topped the rise and came into the pass. The bullets ricocheted off into the distance, noisier than they were dangerous. That didn't matter to him. He just wanted to keep them back where they couldn't do any harm.

His heart sank when he saw the bright flash from the pass. One of the Indians had taken the time to get a signal mirror out and try to locate the rest of the war party. The timed flashes were designed to attract attention—and they did.

To his left, back along the road they had originally taken to get to the fort, Slocum saw an answering signal. It might have been the same party of six Cheyenne that Evangeline had spotted earlier or it might be others. It hardly mattered. They were in a position to cut them off before they reached the safety of the fort.

Evangeline was riding for the front gate. Slocum picked up the pace. His pony responded valiantly. Out of the corner of his eye he saw the six Cheyenne braves they had seen earlier begin to gallop toward the fort. This was about the most foolhardy thing Slocum had ever seen. They would be riding straight into the muzzles of the cavalry's rifles. A trooper might not be too accurate; ammunition for practice was scarce and government budgets didn't allow too much target training. But with enough troopers firing, they had to hit something, or just come close. Slocum was past caring if the Indians were ever sent back to Oklahoma. He just wanted them off his trail.

"John! Hurry! The gate—"

Evangeline had reached the gate and was waiting. She waved. He wondered why the hell she didn't ride on in.

Then he wondered why the hell the soldiers weren't helping them. A few well-placed rounds would have turned the Indians' attack and let both him and Evangeline waltz on into the post without any trouble.

He reached the woman's side and stared past her into the fort and knew the answer. Fort Desolation was well named. The garrison had been abandoned.

9

"Get in, get inside!" Slocum shouted. He slapped the rump of Evangeline's horse to urge it into the fort. The garrison might be gone but the walls, needing repair even as they did, were better protection than standing outside.

The woman obeyed. Slocum hit the ground running and let his horse rush past him as he struggled with the heavy wooden gates. One slammed shut. The other resisted his efforts to get it moving. He bent over, put his shoulder to the corner of the gate and used his strong legs to shove as hard as he could. The ponderous weight began to swing. Faster and faster it moved, eventually closing with a dull thud. It took Slocum only seconds to pull the heavy locking bar through the steel guides to secure the gate.

"My rifle. Toss it to me. The Cheyenne are still coming after us."

Slocum didn't see how they were going to get out of this alive, but if he had to die, he was going to take a few of the Indians with him. Evangeline handed him his rifle. He tried to remember how many rounds he had fired back in the pass, how many remained. Slocum gave up. He'd fire until he ran out of ammo. Then he would die. It was that simple.

He poked the rifle through a gun loop to the side of the gate. He saw a Cheyenne warrior pull to a halt out in the road leading into the fort. Slocum got off a quick shot that spooked the brave's horse. At this range he didn't think he had done any real damage to either horse or rider. When the brave turned and gestured obscenely in his direction, Slocum knew the man was unhurt.

"More ammo. Get the ammunition from my saddle-bags," he called to Evangeline. "I need to reload."

"I'll do it for you. I know how. William showed me."

He handed her the rifle and drew his six-shooter. Slocum pushed his forehead against the hole in the wall and watched the Cheyenne braves forming into ranks. He wondered if they would try circling the fort, looking for a spot he couldn't defend. Once they found it, they'd be over the walls in a flash. Whoever had designed Fort Desolation hadn't taken into account the fantastic scaling ability of an Indian warrior.

Slocum had seen a brave, using only two tomahawks, climb a vertical wall and get inside a fort in less than a minute. He looked around, thinking they might be wise to fall back into one of the empty barracks buildings or even the post commander's quarters. If they couldn't keep the Indians from climbing the walls, then they had a better chance of seeing them from a central stronghold as they attacked.

"Here, John. It's ready to fire."

"Where's the commander's office?" Slocum asked. "We can't keep them at bay forever. We're going to have to fall back and find a smaller area to defend."

"That one," she said, pointing to the log house by the flagpole. Slocum looked up the slender pole and blinked.

He should have seen it earlier. No garrison standard fluttered in the slight breeze coming off the mountains. There wasn't even a Union flag. No cavalry outpost was complete without at least one flag.

He ought to have known from the first time he had sighted Fort Desolation that it was empty.

"What are they doing?" Evangeline asked. "Are they attacking yet? They've stopped screaming."

Slocum turned back to the gun loop and looked through. He didn't understand what was happening. The Cheyenne milled around, as if talking it over among themselves what to do.

"They might be waiting for their war chief to give the word," he said. "I've never seen the Cheyenne hold back like this. You can bet that the three I shot up back in the hills want a piece of me."

"Did you kill them?"

"Wounded two of them slightly. I didn't do much more than slow them down, which was all I had counted on doing." Slocum frowned. A pair of riders came up and joined the others, making a band of more than fifteen braves. The newcomers had the eagle feathers and raiment of chiefs. They pointed repeatedly at the fort and argued with the others.

"They're still not attacking," Evangeline said, looking over Slocum's shoulder. "What are we going to do?"

"Prepare for when they do attack. The only thing they can be talking over is the best way of coming at us. They're no fools. They've got to know the fort is empty."

"There are a couple cannon on the parade ground," Evangeline said uncertainly. "Can we use them?"

"Not unless the powder and shells are nearby. I don't think we've got the time to find them and load the cannon."

Slocum wasn't sure firing one or even two cannonade was the answer. That tactic worked best against marching lines of men. The Indians were too mobile a target. The exploding shells might spook their horses, but the effect would be temporary. He wished for an entire regiment of bluecoats to come marching out of their mess hall, singing and ready for battle.

Only wind whistling through the deserted buildings greeted his ears.

"Get to the commander's office. I'll see if there are more rifles stored somewhere. We need all the ammo and weapons we can lay our hands on." He handed Evangeline his Winchester and raced off to find the armory. He walked quickly past the adjutant's office and the officer's mess, then found the small, sturdy building just beyond the parade ground. The lock on the door had been pried off.

Slocum stuck his head inside and found what he had suspected. The racks for the military carbines were empty. A few kegs of black powder were still inside, as was a case of ammunition that didn't fit either his Colt Navy or the Winchester. He hefted it anyway, thinking he could set fire to it and send bullets sailing everywhere. It wasn't much, but it might wound one or two of the Cheyenne.

"Any luck?" Evangeline asked when he dropped the heavy case on the commander's porch.

"Not much. I'm going back to get a keg of black powder. If nothing else, we can blow them to kingdom come when they come after us. Find something to use as fuse. I didn't see any in the storeroom."

He returned with the twenty-pound keg of black powder just as Evangeline was finishing a long, thin fuse made from muslin.

"The sheets on the bed were all I could find that might burn," she said almost apologetically. "I hope no one minds."

"Let's hope the Indians will mind." Slocum set to filling pouches in the makeshift fuse with enough powder to keep it burning. He placed the keg just inside the door, where they could fall back and light it when the Cheyenne overran them. The explosion would kill a few braves and both of them—and that was the way Slocum wanted it.

He knew what the Indians would do to a white woman, and he wasn't too keen on what they might do to him if they captured him. Better to die fighting than to find out new and horrible Cheyenne tortures.

"When is it going to start?" the woman asked after ten minutes. "They weren't that far away. If they were going to sneak in after dark, they would have started by now."

Slocum looked out the window and saw the solid red disk of the sun dipping below the mountains. Twilight slowly stalked the land and cast long, gray shadows. Any of them might hide a dozen Cheyenne braves. Slocum grew increasingly restive. He didn't know why they hadn't launched an all-out attack earlier. There was no question that the garrison was gone and that he and Evangeline were sitting ducks.

"Why, John?" she asked.

He shrugged. He didn't have any idea why the Indians hadn't come after them immediately. The war chief had talked the others out of it. But why? It didn't make any sense, not after he had winged the two braves in the pass. That should have made them hot for his scalp.

"We need food. I'll see what I can rustle up."

"I'll tend to the horses. The stable must have enough fodder to keep them happy, even if the company tried to take everything with it when the soldiers left."

"Where do you think they went?" Evangeline wrung her hands together. "William didn't say a word about the Army recalling him."

Slocum looked around and tried to figure it out. He couldn't. It was almost as if the soldiers had simply left one afternoon and had never returned.

"Keep a watch out for Indians," he said. "I'll be back in a few minutes." He tended the grateful horses, giving them oats from a large bin and then seeing that they were properly watered. He brushed their coats until they shone, all the while thinking hard. Nothing made any sense. The Army didn't just abandon an outpost. And Cheyennes on the run from their reservation didn't leave behind witnesses.

Slocum finished and went to the stockade wall, rifle in hand. He climbed a ladder to a sentry post and peered into the night. He thought he saw movement but couldn't be sure. Finally deciding it was his own imagination, he made a slow circuit of the post. The walls were intact, though sadly in need of repair. Fort Desolation wasn't the best kept in the world, but it was far from being the worst. But where were the horse soldiers? Where was Evangeline Dunbar's brother?

Answers weren't coming to him. He dropped from the wall and returned to the commander's quarters. The smell of food cooking made his mouth water. He entered carefully, not wanting to spook Evangeline. The woman's hand was resting on the derringer. When she saw it wasn't a Cheyenne, she relaxed and went back to stirring the savory mixture in the cast iron cooking pot.

"It's not much," she said, "but I found a few dried vegetables over in the mess. I put some of the jerky we'd brought in, too, and I think it's tenderizing enough to eat. I never could abide it all tough and salty."

Slocum didn't mention the maggots that often gnawed away at the jerky. He settled down at the table and ate with relish. Only when they had finished off the entire pot between them, did he speak.

"I don't know where your brother is—or the others— but we seem to be safe enough for the moment."

"I wonder why," she murmured to herself. Then her dancing, bright eyes fixed on him and an impish grin curled the corners of her lovely mouth. "If there's no immediate danger, why don't we turn in? We can both use the—rest."

He knew she wasn't talking about going to bed to sleep. It was risky not keeping a guard awake all night. Slocum thought about it for a moment, then returned her wicked smile. The Cheyenne hadn't attacked when they had the upper hand. There wasn't any reason to suppose the braves would choose the middle of the night to set upon them.

Fort Desolation was deserted—and all theirs.

Evangeline read the look and rose gracefully from the table. "I'll be outside waiting for you," she said.

"Outside? What? Why?" That was as far as Slocum got before she slipped out the door. He frowned. Where did she think she was going? The commanding officer's bed looked perfect to him. There was a soft feather comforter on top and the mattress beneath it was firm enough for anything they might want to do.

"John," came her soft call. "Come out and catch me— if you can!"

The challenge set fire to his loins. He stood in the doorway and scanned the parade ground for her. Slight movement near the enlisted men's barracks drew him. He went into the night cautiously, hand on his six-shooter. Evangeline might like playing games, but he wasn't going to stumble over a Cheyenne brave by accident.

"Here, John, over here," she called. A white fluttering caught his attention. She had slipped off her dress and was waving it. The white was her undergarment. Like a ghost, Evangeline drifted away. "Catch me if you caaaan—"

He hurried now and scooped up her dress. There wasn't any reason to leave her garments strewn around the post. They might have to leave in a hurry. He didn't think Evangeline wanted to ride out buck naked. But then, Slocum couldn't really tell.

The woman left a trail of clothing for him to follow. He gathered it up as he went and finally came to a halt in the middle of the parade field. Evangeline stood by the flagpole, her arms and legs wrapped about the smooth staff. She moved up and down it, stimulating herself.

"John, I want you now. Come here. Come and show me that big gun of yours."

He walked toward her slowly. Evangeline was a pale apparition moving through the darkness. Just before he could reach out and touch her, she darted away, rushing toward the cast iron cannon a few feet away. Evangeline jumped atop it and straddled the barrel. She rocked back and forth, a look of delight on her face.

"This is so good," she said, "but it'll be better when you join me. Hurry, John, hurry!"

He was almost ripping off his gun belt and coat and vest and trousers. He kept his eyes on Evangeline's wondrously naked body. She seemed to drift in and out of focus, a lovely, tormenting pale ghost promising eventual paradise. He got to the cannon and reached for her, almost expecting to find nothing but cold iron. His hand brushed across a warm, trembling breast.

"Yes," she hissed. "Now, John. I want it all now."

She thrust her chest out, and he found he had a double handful of breasts. She shifted from side to side to position them just right. He squeezed down on the succulent mounds and felt the hardness springing to life at the tips. He bent over and sucked on first one and then the other coppery nipple. Every light caress with his tongue, every hard suck, every taunting kiss brought even more life to her breasts. They pulsed and throbbed with desire, and Evangeline cooed like a dove. Her hands stroked over his lank black hair and kept him close.

"It's so good, John, so damned good. I've never felt this hot before. Do something about it. I need you to do more."

Slocum didn't need any urging on this score. He wiggled and got free of his long johns. Evangeline looked down from her perch on the cannon barrel and laughed.

"What's so funny?" he asked, startled.

"I was thinking of all the soldiers on the parade ground standing at attention. None ever looked finer!"

She tugged at him until he took a step closer. Evangeline slid back and forth a couple times to give him the idea, then slipped down the smooth cannon barrel until her long legs were on either side of his body. Then Slocum found himself surrounded by clinging moist female flesh. He reached down and cupped her buttocks. With this fleshy grip, he began bouncing her up and down. He felt himself sliding in and out of her in a way he couldn't describe.

He didn't have to describe it. All he had to do was enjoy it. The fires burned down his length and into his loins. His balls began contracting as Evangeline moved around him. She did things with her inner muscles that made him think he was a cow being milked. She squeezed and caressed and stroked and never once used her fingers.

She bent forward and kissed him so passionately she bruised his lips. He felt her breasts flattening against his chest. A cool night wind whipped across the deserted parade ground and sucked away the love sweat forming on their bodies. Slocum had thought she was crazy to go off the way she had. Now he couldn't think of a time when he had been more aroused.

Swinging the brunette back and forth, bouncing her up and down on his fleshy shaft, Slocum slowly reached the point where he wasn't able to control himself any longer.

"More, John. Give me more!"

She was adamant but Slocum's body was betraying him. His balls tightened even more. He felt the hot tide rising inside. Then he exploded just as the cannon might.

Evangeline threw back her head and let out a howl of pent-up desire that would have made any lovelorn coyote jealous. She thrashed about, impaled on his staff, bouncing and twisting and cramming her hips down as hard as she could into his groin. By the time he couldn't go on any more, Evangeline was sliding down his body. She settled on her knees in front of him.

She looked up, her brown eyes glowing with an inner light.

"It's never been this good, John. Never. I don't want it to ever end."

"Let's hope it doesn't have to," he said. But he was already straining to hear the tiny creaks and settling noises made by the fort in the night. Danger was everywhere. The Cheyenne hadn't attacked. The horse soldiers were still missing. And he had no idea what they were going to do next.

Evangeline showed him. After they had finished again, he scooped her up and carried her back to the commanding officer's quarters. It wasn't until just before dawn that they both fell into a deliciously exhausted sleep.

10

Slocum and Evangeline awoke with a start when the unearthly howling began. For a moment Slocum thought it was part of his own dream of the woman sitting out on the cannon. It took several seconds for him to realize Evangeline was sitting bolt upright in bed next to him, as startled as he was.

"There," she said in a husky voice. "Did you hear it, too?" The words weren't out of her mouth when another inhuman shriek rent the still air. Slocum grabbed his six-shooter and swung out of bed. He fumbled for a few seconds getting into his trousers. Going around buck naked as he hunted for whatever had made that noise didn't sit well with him. If he was going to die, he wanted to do it with some shred of decency.

"John, wait. Don't leave me here alone. I don't want to let my imagination run wild."

"Get dressed," he told her. He checked his rifle and

made sure the magazine was filled. As he worked, the howling continued, louder, closer. The Indians often tried to spook their enemies, but this wasn't like any Cheyenne call he had ever heard. It was shriller, more insistent—and it carried the decaying whiff of insanity with it.

"Is it an animal in pain?" she asked as she struggled into her dress and shoes.

"Take this," he said, passing the rifle to her. "You know how to use it. And no, I don't think it's any animal. In spite of the sound, that's coming from a human throat."

Slocum shuddered when the hideous inhuman shrieks turned into a mocking laughter. There wasn't any reason for him to doubt that the laughter was at his expense. Anyone hearing this god-awful sound had to be scared.

"What are we going to do?" Evangeline asked, rifle clutched in her hands. Slocum saw that the woman was shaking hard. This might have been the first time he had seen her really frightened. He didn't blame her. The high-pitched ululation that rose to greet the moon was rubbing his nerves raw, too.

"The sound is coming from inside the compound. I don't think it's any doing of the Indians."

"But who—"

"I don't know," he said, keeping her from thinking too much about the kind of man capable of making such a noise. The cavalry had pulled out. There wasn't much reason to think that they might have left someone behind—unless that someone was crazier than a loon. Slocum had seen his share of lunatics and knew they were unpredictable and could fly into murderous rages. The notion that it was a crazy man sharing the post with them was bolstered by the way the Cheyenne had refused to come after them earlier. Like most Indian tribes, they were more than a little frightened by madmen and gave them wide berth.

"Stay close behind me, but not too close. If he jumps me, I want you to be able to use the rifle."

"But I might hit you."

Slocum looked at the woman. "I know. Aim carefully," he said. Slocum pushed open the front door to the commander's quarters and let his eyes adjust to the moonlit terrain. He saw nothing moving around the parade grounds or over at the mess. The enlisted men's barracks was on the other side of the adjutant's office and the storerooms. He glanced at the keg of black powder by the door and wondered if he could use it to flush out the howling madman. He couldn't see any way of doing it. After another series of the throat-tearing cries, total silence descended on the compound.

"Now," he said. He moved through the shadows, a silent brother with the darkness. Slocum kept moving when he got to the edge of the commander's cabin and slid into moonlight. He waited for a moment to see if the howling would resume. That would mean he was being watched. When nothing came, he moved quickly toward the adjutant's office.

Behind him he heard Evangeline's soft footsteps. He wasn't happy having a scared woman carrying a rifle at his back, but he wasn't going to leave her alone. If anything, that might have been why the unearthly bellows had been sounded.

"Could this be Quentin's doing?" asked Evangeline.

"What?" The question startled him. He hadn't thought about the men on Evangeline's trail for some time. He had been too busy fighting off the Cheyenne—and making love to the lovely woman.

"Quentin Magee. You remember him. My papa's business partner. The one who tried to kidnap me."

Slocum said nothing. This was the first time he had heard the name Magee. He had thought Quentin was the man's last name. There was a whale of a lot Evangeline wasn't telling him, but this wasn't the time to go into the details.

"He's ahead, maybe behind the barracks." Slocum dropped to his knees and looked around the corner of the adjutant's office. He saw nothing moving at ground level, but he knew the best way of keeping control of an area was to seek the high ground. On the barracks roof he saw small movements in the shadow.

"Do you want the rifle?" Evangeline saw the movement, too.

Slocum thought fast. "No," he said, coming to a decision. "I'll take him without shooting him." Slocum had questions he needed answers for and capturing the howling lunatic alive was the only way he was likely to get them.

He shoved his Colt Navy back into the cross-draw holster and moved toward the barracks, darting from shadow to shadow. The bright light from the almost full moon gave some cover but forced him to reveal himself when he crossed large stretches of the open compound. He finally sidled up to the barracks, his back against the cold wood planking. Just above him on the roof squatted the man responsible for giving him and Evangeline such a turn. He saw the man's boots poking over the edge.

Still wary, Slocum moved to one side and chanced a quick look up. A slow smile crossed his face. He had been right to be so cagey. Only a pair of boots rested on the roof. The man who had worn them was trying to get away.

Slocum drew his pistol and went in the other direction. He stood under a drainpipe as a man scampered down it. When the man's bare feet touched the top of a water barrel, Slocum jammed his pistol into the small of the man's back.

"Move and I'll cut you in half," he said in a tone that brooked no argument.

"No, I give up, don't kill me!" The man threw up his hands and fell backward off the tottering barrel. Slocum stepped out of the way and let him fall hard to the ground.

"Get up," he said, sighting down the barrel of his Colt. "If you don't, I'll plug you. You went and disturbed my rest. I've shot men for a lot less."

"No, don't." The disheveled man cowered on the ground. "Don't hurt me. I didn't mean nothing by it."

"If he doesn't drill you, I will," said Evangeline. She aimed the rifle squarely at the man.

"She's got a mean streak in her," Slocum said. "I'd start trying to explain what the hell's going on. Why were you trying to scare us?"

"They're all gone. They done rode off and left me. Gone, and me the only survivor."

"Survivor of what?" Slocum walked around and got a better look at the man's face. He shuddered. The deep craters spoke of a bout with smallpox. Not many survived that dread disease, but those who did were scarred like this man.

"The pox. It came rushing down on us, God's divine retribution for lives of sin, and it kilt damn near everyone! I lived, but when I came out of the fever, the rest was long gone."

"Smallpox?" Evangeline said in a chocked voice. "What about my brother? What of William Dunbar?"

"Who?"

"Lieutenant William Dunbar," she said firmly, keeping the panic from her voice. Her hands trembled but her words were level. "He was one of the three company commanders at this fort."

"Never heard of him. Nobody here by that name. Don't know what you mean." The man started sobbing gently.

"He's lying," Evangeline said. "William *was* here. He had to be. He wouldn't desert."

"Calm down," Slocum said. "There's a quick way to get to the truth of the matter." He kicked the man on the ground to his feet and herded him toward the adjutant's office. Inside Slocum made the pockmarked man sit in a corner.

"The pay records!" cried Evangeline. "Of course. Those will show if William received his monthly pay."

"Go on and look through the books," Slocum said. "That one looks to be a ledger of some sort."

Evangeline took a thick, dusty volume from a shelf. She

settled in the straight-backed chair behind the desk and started leafing through the pages. She finally looked up and said, "It's the paymaster's record book, and William drew his pay every month for the past eight months."

"When was the last entry?"

"A little over a month ago. He was due to be paid a week back, but there's no sign anyone was paid."

"So the garrison has been deserted for over a week," Slocum mused. He turned to their gibbering prisoner. "Tell us about it. What happened here?"

"Smallpox! It was the pox what wiped the fort out. Kilt everyone, leastwise those that couldn't or didn't run."

Evangeline began to fidget. Slocum shook his head and said, "The man's lying. I looked around the post earlier when I was waiting for the Cheyenne to attack. I saw the post cemetery outside the walls. There's not more than a dozen graves there. Most of the plots have the look of being old."

"Mass graves, burned all them bodies up to get rid of the infection," the man babbled.

"Who are you?" asked Evangeline.

"Sergeant Ben Madsen, at your service," he said. Slocum shoved him back to the floor to keep him from springing to attention.

"You stay down on the floor where we can see you," Slocum said. "Is there a listing for a Sergeant Ben Madsen in the paymaster's book?"

He didn't need Evangeline's quiet "no" to come to the conclusion their prisoner was one lying snake in the grass.

"What are we going to do, John? We can't just shoot him, and I certainly do not want to share this fort with him."

"I'll take care of it. There's a small stockade behind the mess. He'll be safe enough there."

"In a cell?" Evangeline wasn't sure she wanted even this for their captive. His odd gurgling and cries still scared her.

"He'll be fine. I'll check the cell first to be sure he hasn't tampered with it."

"Hate boxes. Don't lock me up. Can't stand it. The old sarge can't take it. Don't do this to me."

Slocum grabbed the man by his filthy collar and pulled him along. He shoved Madsen into the center cell, checked the hinges, floor, and small barred window and finally locked the door. Madsen cowered in a corner, cooing to himself.

"Are you sure this is the right thing to do, John?" Evangeline asked the instant he left the small jailhouse.

"You want to gun him down? He looks like he's had smallpox but there's no telling when. Those scars might be years old. The one thing I don't doubt is that Madsen's not in his right mind."

"You make it sound like a boon."

"It kept the Cheyenne from attacking us," Slocum said. He explained that they must have ridden by earlier and heard the awful howling sounds from within. "They won't enter unconsecrated burial grounds, either. The way I see it, Madsen is our ace in the hole."

"What are we going to do?"

"You're going to try to get some sleep. Me, I think I'm going outside to explore a mite."

"What!"

"Why not? The Cheyenne may have moved on. There's not much cause for them to stay around and listen to a lunatic baying at the moon. It scares them more than it did us."

"What are you really looking for?"

Slocum considered this. He finally said, "The troopers who were here at the fort left not more than a couple weeks back. I want to find some trace of them."

He didn't tell Evangeline but curiosity was eating him up inside. Horse soldiers didn't just abandon their post. Ten or twenty percent might just walk away during any given year. The Union Army wasn't that good at keeping their soldiers in rank, but for an entire garrison to up and leave was a mystery Slocum wanted to solve.

"Don't forget William. He was here. The pay book shows that."

"I won't forget." Slocum kissed her but his mind was already forging ahead to what he had to do. Almost distractedly, he left the woman on the steps of the commander's cabin and went to the back wall of the fort. He found a rung ladder, scaled it and dropped to the far side. From here, he traveled in great looping curves, often coming back over his own trail to be sure he wasn't being followed.

His route took him through the cemetery he had seen from the fort walls. The newest grave was more than six months old. There hadn't been any smallpox epidemic. Sergeant Ben Madsen had lied through his stained, crooked teeth. But this didn't give Slocum any more idea of what had really happened at Fort Desolation.

He considered returning to the fort and Evangeline Dunbar, then decided to keep exploring. She was as safe as a babe in arms. Madsen's demented shrieking would keep the Cheyenne away for the time being. He wanted more information about the former soldiers at the post. Wiggling along on his belly brought him to the perimeter of the Cheyenne camp. A half dozen fires guttered. The wan firelight and the silver rays from the moon showed a dozen or more braves sitting upright, their heads resting against their raised knees. The snoring was loud enough to cover any small sounds he might make.

Stealing one of the Indian ponies was almost too easy. Slocum hadn't ridden bareback in a long time, but having a sturdy horse under him was far better than remaining on foot. He walked the animal away from the others, then mounted and got the feel of the horse.

By the time he reached the road leading back toward the desert stretches on the far side of the mountains, Slocum and the horse had adjusted to one another. He rode at the edge of the road, looking for any sign that a cavalry troop had passed by.

He rode for miles but found no trace of the missing troopers.

Just a bit after sunrise, he reined back and decided to return to the fort. He wasn't sure how he was going to get back inside, but the Cheyenne weren't going to camp outside forever. They had better things to do than listen to a madman howl at the moon like a rabid coyote.

"Get to the fort, wait till sundown, then find Evangeline," he said, thinking out loud. He patted the horse's neck to soothe her, but the horse refused to be mollified. Slocum dismounted and led the horse to a patch of grass. The horse kept jerking her head about.

This was ample warning for Slocum. Listening hard, he heard the rumble of wagon wheels and the sound of men singing.

He pulled the horse back into a grove of cottonwoods and found a small artesian well for the horse to water at. This kept the animal occupied while the wagons came rumbling into view. Slocum hung back and watched, trying to decide who the hell these men were.

He was going to let the party pass him by when one riding scout spotted him. Rather than let the armed men come to him, Slocum waved and stepped out. He put on his friendliest smile and called to them.

"Howdy. Where you folks going?"

"We're heading on over to Mule Head City," the scout said. He hushed up when a man in rugged clothing rode over. The man's checked shirt had seen better days, as had his boots. His toes poked out through the leather and the soles were well nigh gone, but there wasn't any mistaking this to be the party's leader.

"What you doin' sneakin' about like that?" the tall, bearded man asked Slocum.

"Just being careful," Slocum said. "There's a large band of Cheyenne up ahead. They got Fort Desolation surrounded. If that's your destination, you're riding straight into the jaws of hell."

"That's not where we're going," the man snapped. "We're a tad lost."

"We're looking for Mule Head City," the scout said, looking embarrassed. "I got us on the wrong road a ways back."

"Don't rightly know where this town is you're looking for," admitted Slocum, "but you'd probably do well to turn around and try to find where you took the wrong turn."

"That's what I've been tellin' this pig-headed son of a bitch," the leader said. "We got track to lay. Each day my men sit on their butts, the company loses five hundred dollars. We need to get rails down from Mule Head City to Cedar City to meet up with track just coming over the pass there."

"You railroad men?"

"Born and bred," the scout said. "And I'll be damn happy when I get them to the end of their line."

"Injuns?" the leader asked. "Just what we need." He cast a cold eye on Slocum, as if scrutinizing his soul for any tarnish. "You wouldn't be lyin' about this, would you?"

"No reason to," Slocum said. "You might want to ride just a few miles on and check it out for yourself. I was lucky to get away from them myself. I was hoping to find the cavalry troop stationed there at the fort. You haven't seen any blue coats, have you?"

"We ain't seen nary a soul till you popped up," the leader said. He spat and then turned and motioned. "Get them wagons turned around. We're goin' back. The cutoff for Mule Head City can't be more'n ten miles back."

He didn't say another word to Slocum as he wheeled his horse and saw to getting his wagons turned. In the backs of the wagons Slocum saw heavy iron prybars, sledgehammers, and enough spikes to lay a hundred miles of track. Most of the men in the wagons were Chinese and jabbered among themselves in a singsong Slocum couldn't understand.

"Don't reckon I'm going to get paid for this job," the scout said. "You serious about them Injuns?"

"Dead serious," Slocum said. "And you haven't seen any cavalry?"

"Not a hair." With that the scout put his heels into his horse's sides and galloped to catch up with the furious leader of the track crew. Slocum stood and watched until the last of the dust had settled. He heaved a sigh. There just wasn't any telling who he would run into along this road. From the map, it was the most desolate land on the face of the earth, but he had already run into a railroad crew and enough Cheyenne fresh off their reservation to populate a small town.

He rubbed his belly when it began to growl and decided it was time for breakfast. He went hunting and dropped a small rabbit with his thick-bladed hunting knife. He skinned and cooked the animal and was finishing when he heard more horses in the distance.

Slocum smiled wryly. The railroad crew must have gotten on the wrong road again and come full circle. He peered into the distance and saw a dozen men on horses. Not a one sported feathers or any other paraphernalia worn by the Cheyenne. He went back to the road and waited for the first rider to come up.

The rider frowned when he saw him but kept coming.

"You get turned around again?" Slocum asked.

"We didn't get turned around," the man said.

Slocum waited for the heavily laden wagons to rumble back into sight. When he saw that the wagons weren't coming, he sucked in his breath and tensed up.

"Don't go gettin' any damn fool ideas, mister." The rider had a shotgun out and aimed directly at Slocum. "I reckon the boss will be wantin' to talk to you."

"The boss?"

"Mr. Magee! Over here. I got me a stranger."

Magee. Slocum's heart leaped into his throat. He had been captured by Quentin Magee's men without so much as a fight.

11

"Reach for that six-shooter of yours and I'll smear your damned guts all over the countryside," the rider said in a wintry voice. His finger turned white as he tightened on the twin triggers of the double-barreled shotgun.

Slocum looked around, trying to figure a way of getting out of his predicament. He didn't find one. He had waited too long. A half dozen riders formed a semicircle around him. Most had their hands on their six-shooters and were ready to draw. Even if they weren't eager for a fight, Slocum saw no way of outrunning them. The captured Indian pony was still back in the stand of trees. It would take him precious seconds to run and mount. By that time he'd weigh twice as much as he did now from all the lead shot that would be pumped into his back.

"What do we have here?" asked a thin man with a bushy handlebar mustache. "Can this be the oaf she got to squire her to this desolate part of the world?"

Slocum stared at the dapper man and wondered if this was Quentin Magee. If so, Slocum wasn't quite sure what he had expected. This man was well dressed in a stylish coat and trousers, if a bit dirty from the trail. His thick black mustache drooped a mite at the ends and his forehead was caked with dirt where the trail dust had settled into his heavily oiled hair. A bit of sprucing up and the man might be considered debonair by San Francisco society standards.

But what rocked Slocum the most was how young the man was. He might be ten years younger than Slocum. This was hardly the kind of man to go into business with Evangeline's father.

"Who else would be out here, boss?" asked the man with the shotgun.

"We did run into those railroad idiots."

"Their scout had gotten them lost," spoke up another man. "They were on their way to Mule Head City."

Magee sniffed derisively. "Such quaint names, though appropriate, I have no doubt." He studied Slocum for a few seconds, then asked, "Where is Evie?"

It took Slocum a few seconds to realize the man meant Evangeline.

"She's where you won't find her. You tried to kidnap her twice. You won't get the chance again." He had considered trying to bluff his way out but there was a hint of cruelty in Magee's dark eyes that bothered Slocum. He had seen it before in cold-blooded killers. Nothing would stop him once he set his mind to a chore.

Capturing Evangeline Dunbar was obviously his sole reason for coming to Desolation Point.

"Such false bravado. You know there are ways of making you reveal the information I need." Magee took a white linen handkerchief from his pocket and spat into it. He wrapped up the spittle as if it were some precious religious relic and put it back into his pocket. "The Indians are supposed to be good at making a man give up the secrets of his soul. I'm better."

"By the time you weasel it out of me, she'll be long gone," Slocum said with some sincerity.

"That may be so. Give me some reason for keeping you alive."

Slocum saw the pearl-handled pistol stuck into Magee's belt and the way his hand twitched slightly.

"If I tell you, you'll kill me anyway."

"Probably," Magee said, "but it's more reasonable to keep you alive until I find that irritating woman. That way I'll know that you've told the truth. It is so vexing to kill someone and find that he's sold me a bill of goods."

One of the riders dismounted and relieved Slocum of his Colt Navy and the knife sheathed at the small of his back. Try as he might, Slocum couldn't see any way of escaping. The riders circling him were too attentive. Even if they hadn't been, the man with the shotgun kept an eagle eye on him until he was tied securely to the back of his captured pony.

"What sort of man goes riding about this wretched countryside on an Indian mount?" Magee spoke to himself, as if trying to figure out Slocum's part in everything.

"What'll you do with her when you get to Fort Desolation?" asked Slocum.

"What? Evie? That is none of your concern," Magee said. He worked on the tips of his thick mustache, getting them into needle points that quickly turned bushy again. "She has led me on such a chase. But then, that's like her. She's got spunk." He rode for a few more minutes and then added, "I hate a woman with spunk."

Slocum rode silently, trying to balance bareback with his hands tied behind his back. He strained to overhear what the others were saying. They must have opinions on their boss' wild goose chase. What manner of man dragged a dozen employees halfway across the country to fetch a woman?

"—get back and see to business," Slocum overheard the

man with the shotgun saying. "The boss is neglecting business something fierce."

"It'll be worth it. When we catch up with the bitch—"

"Don't let *him* hear you calling her that," the man with the shotgun snapped. "You know how he is about her."

"Well, she *is* a bitch. Look at what she done to him back in San Francisco, and he's takin' it. Not like him. Mr. Magee's never took nothing like that off no man. Don't see a reason for him to take it off any woman."

Slocum tried to spy on what the others were saying but didn't get the chance. They were riding straight into the Cheyenne camp. He had warned the railroad crew. He had given some clue to Magee about what lay ahead at Fort Desolation but the man obviously thought he was lying, in spite of the evidence. Who rode around southwestern Utah on an Indian mount—except an Indian? Magee seemingly chose to ignore Slocum's mode of transportation.

"What's got you so riled up?" the man with the shotgun asked Slocum. "You're looking to be as nervous as a long-tailed cat in a rocking chair factory."

"Cheyenne," Slocum said. "I tried to tell you before. There's a whole war party of Cheyenne up ahead."

"Yeah, and my Aunt Tillie's a sword swallower," the man scoffed. "Why'd a bunch of renegade Injuns choose a cavalry outpost to camp? That don't make good sense."

Slocum shrugged it off and went back to trying to twist the ropes around his wrist into a more comfortable spot. Blood leaked from the abrasions and turned the hemp strands wet. As it dried, it would begin tightening. He'd never be able to work free then. His only chance was to slip his hands free now and continue riding as if he was still tied up. When Magee and his men ran into the Cheyennes Slocum intended to make his break then.

But what could he do about Evangeline? She was still in the fort waiting for him. Slocum quickly forgot that problem. If he didn't escape Magee, all the worrying in the world wasn't going to help the lovely woman.

"Hey, boss, there's someone in the road up ahead. Looks like it might be an Injun."

Slocum strained to get his hands free. The ropes refused to give. He was going to have to make his break for freedom when the Cheyenne attacked.

"Ain't no Indian," said the man Slocum had pegged as the foreman. "Ain't nobody a'tall. It's just a coat hung on a juniper."

Slocum's eyes widened when he saw the jacket. It was a cavalry sergeant's but of its owner there wasn't a trace. He wondered if this might have belonged to the crazy man he had caught howling at the moon inside the fort.

"No sign of Injuns anywhere, boss," came the lead rider. "The fort's just up ahead. What we gonna tell the blue coats when we get there?"

"The truth. We tell them we're looking for a woman."

Slocum wondered if Magee knew Evangeline's brother was stationed at Fort Desolation. From the way the dapper man spoke, he didn't have an inkling. That was even more puzzling. Magee was acting as if he had lost a prized possession and nothing more. It wasn't as if he was trying to stop Evangeline from getting her brother's signature; it was more as if he wanted her back.

"She'll give it to me when I find her," came the words drifting back from the front of the column as they rode. Slocum knew it had been Quentin Magee who had spoken— and it had to be Evangeline he was talking about.

Slocum thought hard as they rode toward the fort. The men abroad the train had acted more as if they wanted information Evangeline had. Magee spoke in the same way. What had he gotten himself into? And what lies had Evangeline Dunbar told him?

"There's nobody in the fort," came the scout's cry. "The gate's standin' wide open. What should I do?"

"Ride on in," came Magee's order. He kept his horse trotting at a steady pace, never breaking stride. He rode into Fort Desolation as if he owned the place. Magee sat stock-still in the middle of the parade ground and slowly wheeled around in a full circle. His cold eyes never missed a detail.

"This is the damnedest thing I ever did see," he said. "You and you, go see if there's anyone left. I want to speak to them. And put him somewhere that he won't be a bother."

The foreman jerked on the rope fastening Slocum's wrists. The sudden yank pulled Slocum off his mount and brought him crashing to the ground. He lay on his side for a moment, the air driven from his lungs. He finally caught his breath again and sat up. The foreman was looking down the barrels of his shotgun.

"You don't want to try anything foolish. Let's just go see if we can salt you away in one of the cavalry's cells. They always have a few iron cages for the rowdy troopers. Never seen a post where they didn't."

"You've seen your share of prison cells, is that it?" asked Slocum.

The foreman laughed harshly. "You might say that. Leastwise, I always got out. That's more'n I can say for you. When the boss finishes looking around this place, he's gonna skin you and hang your hide on the outhouse door to dry."

Slocum said nothing and let the foreman herd him toward the adjutant's office and the jail cells beyond. He paused in the doorway and looked inside the dark cells. He didn't see the crazy sergeant.

"Go on in or I'll just put you out of your misery now."
. The cocking of the hammers on the shotgun convinced Slocum there wasn't anything he could do at the moment. He had looked over the cells and couldn't find any way out of them, but Ben Madsen had escaped the middle cell somehow. Slocum went to it and sat down on the bunk.

"Now that's a good boy. Just like a lamb to the slaughter. I hate it when they put up a struggle." The foreman laughed harshly and banged the cell door shut. He rattled the bars a couple of times to make sure everything was secure, then left.

Slocum spent the next ten minutes rubbing the rope against the ragged edge of the wooden bunk. The hemp strands finally parted. He rubbed the circulation back into his bloodied wrists, then stood and began a careful examination of the cell. Madsen had gotten out. He could, too.

Twenty minutes later Slocum cursed his bad luck. He didn't see how the madman had gotten free. He couldn't believe Evangeline had let the sergeant loose. She had been too frightened of the man.

Slocum went to the barred window and stood on the bunk to look outside. Magee's men had set up camp in the center of the parade ground. Slocum wondered why they didn't stay in the barracks and do their cooking in the mess hall, but he was in no position to ask anyone.

Hands on the cold iron bars, Slocum watched and sniffed at the food being cooked. His belly grumbled. It had been noon when he'd killed the rabbit. He was ready for chow again—and it wasn't likely to be forthcoming. There wasn't any reason for Magee to feed a condemned man.

Slocum growled in anger at his rotten luck. He should never have walked out to warn off Magee's men. This was what he got for doing someone a favor. And the Cheyenne had already left.

"With Evangeline and the crazy man," he said. His thoughts returned to how Madsen had gotten free. Without a key there didn't seem to be any way. The iron bars weren't even scratched. Slocum ran his hands up and down the cold iron, and then he noticed a tiny thread tied on the bottom of the center bar.

Curious, he got it looped around his finger and drew it up. For a moment he simply stared at what was tied on the end. Then he let out a whoop of joy. Lady Luck had decided to smile at him again.

The key tied to the thread opened the cell door. Slocum started out of the cell, then hesitated. He didn't intend on letting Magee's men capture him again, but if they did, he wanted an escape route open again. He replaced the key on its thread. As he dropped it back outside the window, he wondered how many others besides himself and Madsen had used this method of regaining their freedom.

Slocum slipped from the cellblock and moved quietly across the open space between the commander's quarters and the adjutant's office. He looked inside. All Evangeline's belongings were gone. She must have left before Magee had ridden so arrogantly into the fort. That meant she had left soon after he went scouting that morning.

That didn't set well with him. Things were getting more and more complicated and Slocum wanted answers.

He ducked down when he heard boot heels on the porch in front of the cabin. Moving around to the side of the quarters, he looked around. Two of Magee's men sat on the porch and fixed smokes. He heard the hiss of a lucifer and saw the blue spiral of smoke from the red-hot tips of the cigarettes. Dropping to his belly, he wiggled under the porch until he came up under the men. He could hear every word they said.

"—find her soon enough. She can't have gone too far," the foreman was saying. "When the boss catches her, that'll be it." He made a motion of his index finger across his throat.

"What if she doesn't have it with her? He needs it, doesn't he?"

Slocum tried to puzzle out what the man was talking about.

"He might have enough information to find it without her, but it'll help if he gets back everything she stole."

"Can't he find the loot from memory? He saw the map."

"Yeah, but it was only half. Come on, let's make a final check. I want to see how our prisoner's doing."

Slocum knew he didn't have much time. He saw the men's feet shuffle off in the direction of the cells. He wiggled on out from under the porch and walked boldly over to the pile of Magee's equipment. Slocum knelt down and rummaged through until he found his Colt and hunting knife.

He felt dressed again, but he didn't have much time. The foreman would find him missing and all hell would break loose.

He swung a saddle up to his shoulder and started for the corral where the horses were penned. On the way a man called out to him, "Where you going?"

"Boss told me to check the outside of the fort. Damn it," Slocum said. "I ain't had supper yet. You want to ride guard for me so's I can get some grub?"

"Not a chance," the man said, backing off. He was more interested in getting out of work than he was in seeing who he was talking to. Slocum kept walking and found a decent looking horse in the corral. His horse was there, as was the Indian pony he had stolen, but this horse was larger, stronger, and looked as if it could run all night.

Slocum figured it might just have to.

He saddled up and mounted. He tipped his hat in the direction of the man he had just spoken to and said, "Keep some of that grub hot for me. I'll be back in an hour or two."

"Like hell," the man answered. "It gets thrown out if it ain't et."

"Thanks for nothing," Slocum said dryly. He got through the main gates before he heard the foreman's cry of rage. He put his heels to the horse and galloped into the night. There'd be no way they could track him until moonrise. By then Slocum intended to be long gone.

12

The noise from inside Fort Desolation made Slocum smile.
He was glad to cast as much confusion as possible among
Quentin Magee's men. Slocum felt used and lied to and he
didn't hanker on being caught again by the dapper Magee.
The San Francisco dandy would just as soon kill him as
look at him if their paths crossed again. The man's dark,
cold eyes told what went on in his bleak soul.

Slocum rode until the moon rose, bright and round and
almost full. He slowed his pace and began to circle a mite.
He didn't want to stay on the road. That would give Magee's
men too good a chance to catch up with him. Also, Slocum
wasn't sure where the Cheyenne braves had gone. He had
counted on them being outside the fort when Magee rode
in. Wherever they were, they hadn't ridden far.

That brought him to Evangeline Dunbar. She was gone,
too. The thought of the woman's perfidy made him begin
to seethe. He hated being lied to. Slocum wasn't sure if she

had told him the truth at any point or about anything. The notion that she needed her brother's signature to keep the family business from being stolen by Quentin Magee was an outright lie. Slocum had heard the way Magee spoke of Evangeline—Evie he had called her. Their relationship had been something more than just business.

And Magee's foreman had mentioned a map. To what? The southern Utah mountains were loaded with legends and tall tales of lost mines and buried treasure. Most of it didn't amount to a hill of beans, as far as Slocum was concerned. Following the elusive trail of hidden gold was a good way to end up dead from starvation. Better to join the railroad crew and lay a few miles of track to stay alive. That was at least honest labor and more likely to leave a few dollars in your pocket than scouring these miserable hills for something left behind scores of years back.

Slocum dismounted and went through the saddlebags on the gear he had stolen. His belly grumbled when he found a can of beans and two of peaches. He used his knife to open the beans and wolfed them down. He looked longingly at the peaches but decided to let them be. He might need their sustenance and liquid later. For all the springs and streams in these mountains, Slocum knew there were long dry stretches. He wasn't all that familiar with Desolation Point, Utah, but the very name told him this was no country to be lost in.

He lay back and watched the moon climb across the sky. He sat bolt upright when he thought he heard a baying. He settled back when he decided it was a timber wolf coming down from the high country and not the crazy Sergeant Ben Madsen imitating a coyote. An hour passed and Slocum got a little sleep. When he awoke, everything had worked itself out in his mind.

He wasn't going to ride off. He didn't have two coins to rub together. Beside being flat ass broke, Evangeline had lied to him. That rankled more than any nettle under the skin ever could.

"Where would she go?" he asked himself. He tried to picture the lay of the land in his mind. He hadn't had much chance to look around Fort Desolation after they had arrived, other than to check for a Cheyenne attack. Still, the road where he had been captured by Magee wasn't a likely place for Evangeline to have gone. The Cheyenne probably took off and went on down the road in the other direction. She wouldn't follow them. She had been too frightened.

That left only the area to the north of the fort. Slocum remembered a low pass matching the one to the south through which they had approached Fort Desolation originally. Evangeline wouldn't retrace her steps. She would press on—and Slocum bet she had gone north.

He mounted and started for the area north of the fort. It took the better part of three hours of careful riding to get to the low pass, but the brilliant moonlight immediately revealed the woman's trail.

Slocum dismounted and studied the spoor. Evangeline had ridden through and left part of her shirt hanging on a prickly shrub. The bright, shining part he had first noticed was a button sewn to the fabric. He walked a few yards up into the pass and saw faint markings that might have been left by the woman's horse. He was on the right track—and she wasn't too far ahead of him.

Slocum was dog tired by the time the moon sank and the sun rose, but he was happy with the night's ride. In a secluded valley below ran a sluggish river, and camped beside it was Evangeline Dunbar. Slocum wanted to ride directly to her and demand to know why she had lied to him ever since their first meeting, but he held back.

Walking his horse down the steep trail into the valley, he bided his time and went over everything in his mind. He didn't think he was walking into a trap because Evangeline thought he was well out of the picture. He saw no way for her to have known Quentin Magee would capture him, but she had wanted to leave him behind. Otherwise, she wouldn't have left the fort as she'd done.

Slocum tied his horse, checked his Colt, and then edged into the clearing. Evangeline knelt beside the stream, struggling to fill the bulky canvas desert bag.

"It helps if you submerge the entire bag," Slocum said.

"Thanks. I—" Evangeline jerked and swung around as if someone had stuck her with a pin. "John!"

"Didn't expect to see me, did you?"

The expression on her face told the story. She had never intended to stay with him. She needed his assistance getting to Desolation Point but hadn't wanted his company after reaching the fort. He wondered if the passion in her lovemaking had been faked, too.

"John, I had to leave the fort. You'd gone and that terrible man was yowling again and—"

"And?" He enjoyed watching Evangeline squirm a mite. She had betrayed him and he wondered how he could best get some measure of revenge on her. His lack of money struck Slocum as a good place to start. Evangeline was rich. She could afford to part with a few dollars before he was on his way. It wouldn't even have to be gold. He'd settle accounts in scrip.

"And the Indians upped and left. They did! I was looking out through the loophole in the wall and saw them riding off. I didn't want to be cooped up in the fort. Not with that crazy man! So I—"

"So you just left without telling me."

"How could I?" Her brown eyes danced. She licked her lips and thrust out her chest just enough to give Slocum some idea what he would be missing if he didn't believe her. This time her physical charms did not work on him. He was too tired and banged up for that. She saw her tactic wasn't working and fell silent, trying to think of something else to appeal to the man she had duped.

"If you'd left a note saying you'd gone, you were afraid Magee would find it and follow you," he finished for her.

"Quentin?"

"You know him," Slocum said coldly. "The man on your trail. The one who wants your map."

Evangeline Dunbar turned pale. Her hand fluttered to her throat, and Slocum thought she was going to faint dead away.

"How did you know about the map?" she asked in a voice almost too low to be heard over the gurgling of the stream. "I never said a word about it. I'm sure!"

"You prattled on and on about your pa," Slocum answered. "You never once gave me a straight answer. One minute he was a merchant, the next a lawyer, and then he was a shipping magnate. I can't even remember all the different professions you gave him—and you were going to inherit whatever it was."

"Quentin was his business partner," she said. He knew it was a lie from the way she mouthed the words.

"Try telling me the truth. What map is it that Magee is after?"

"He told you about the map?"

Slocum said nothing; let her jump to her own wrong conclusions.

"Well," Evangeline said, licking her lips again, this time from nervousness. "It's not true that I had you come here because William had to sign papers."

"You actually have a brother named William?"

"Of course I do. I wouldn't lie about a thing like that."

"And your father?"

Evangeline looked away. "I'm sorry about that, John. There's no inheritance. Fact is, I'm not rich."

"I'd got that idea a while back," he said. "What about the house on Nob Hill?"

Evangeline smiled and shrugged. "It was empty. Who was I to let a perfectly fine home like that go to waste?"

"That's why you didn't have any servants."

"And I suppose you're wondering about the diamond ring I gave those gamblers at the Union Club. It was only costume jewelry. I found it in the house behind a cushion on the divan in the sitting room.''

''You're not rich, you don't have a father leaving you a pile of money, but you do have a brother—and a map.''

''Yes, well, those parts are true. But I wanted to cut you in, John. I did. But the Indians left and the madman began howling. How he got free from his cell I don't know.''

''Cut out the lies, Evie,'' Slocum said nastily. Using the pet name Magee had for her caused her to blanch even more. ''I want to know everything. I've already learned most of it,'' he said, casting out a lie himself to catch the bigger fish of truth, ''but I want to hear it from your lips.''

''You and Quentin—'' The look of horror rising in her brown eyes told Slocum there was no love lost between her and Magee.

''We're not in cahoots,'' Slocum said. ''He didn't treat me too good, truth to tell. I think I can come out of this with more money jingling in my pocket by siding with you rather than with him.''

''He's got a lot of men working for him,'' Evangeline said. ''I'd heard he promised them all a cut of the gold.''

Slocum sighed. So it was just a treasure map. He had hoped it was something more.

''Look, John, there's enough to go around. You and me and William. We can split it three ways. There'll be enough, I promise!''

''Tell me about it.'' Slocum plucked the desert bag from her hands and took a long drink. The cool water puddled in his stomach and reminded him it had been a spell since he'd eaten. He fished out a can of peaches from the saddlebags and started working on them while Evangeline tried to figure out what new lies to tell him.

''William and Quentin were partners. Our father's been dead for years. You were right about them not being in business.''

''Quentin's a considerable bit younger than I'd've thought from the way you talk about him.''

"He's evil. He's a sidewinder. He'll steal every penny you have. That's how he got all he has. Quentin's rich, but he's greedy. He can't ever get enough."

"Never get enough," Slocum mused. The way Evangeline blushed told Slocum that Quentin Magee was more than her brother's business partner. She and the San Francisco dandy had been lovers. Had it been a lover's spat that caused the falling out or was it nothing more than simple greed? Considering the people involved, Slocum was inclined to believe it had been avarice rather than passion gone astray that had started this mess.

"We argued. I—my brother has half the map and I have the other half."

Again, Slocum read more into her words than what Evangeline actually said. She had stolen Magee's half of the map. Her brother had the other half and together they'd gone off to find the fabulous lost treasure. He wondered if it was worth his while to continue or if he ought to climb on his stolen horse and hightail it. Salt Lake City might not be too bad this time of year, even if Young's Lambs of God might be out shooting up heathens.

"Is your brother even in the Army?"

"Of course he is. You don't know how hard it was for him to get transferred to Fort Desolation."

Slocum snorted in derision. Nobody wanted to be assigned to this godforsaken spot. William Dunbar need only to ask and a dozen men would have gladly agreed to swap assignments with him. Buying your way out of an unpleasant command was a way of life in the Army.

"This is how he came across the map in the first place. It's *ours*, John, not Quentin's. We deserve the treasure."

"What treasure is this? A lost gold mine? Do we have to mine it for a year before we see any gold?"

"No," she said, the blush turning to rosy spots on her cheeks. She was excited now, more excited than she had been when they were making love. The thrill of gold excited her more than anything Slocum had ever done for her. "It's Spanish gold."

"Spanish? The conquistadores did come through this part of the country, but why would they leave their gold behind? They shipped most of it back to Spain for their king."

"They didn't leave it, silly," she said. "The Indians stole it from the Spanish and hid it. What use do the Indians have for gold? They prefer silver for their ornaments."

"Indians have been known to make gold ornaments," Slocum said, but he had to agree. The Indians didn't understand the white man's rapacity for the yellow metal.

"They *hid* it, I tell you. And William found the map."

"How'd Magee get involved in this?"

"He horned his way in. He thought, just because he loaned William a little money to do the hunting for the map, that he deserved it. The man is a pig!"

Finding out the details of how Magee had ended up with half the map and William Dunbar the other half didn't interest Slocum. There must have been double-dealing and backstabbing going on all over San Francisco. What was clear was that Evangeline had stolen the map from Magee. Slocum was more interested in finding out if there was any basis for Evangeline's claim about the Spanish gold. Likely there wasn't, he knew. Hidden gold had a way of being discovered and hauled off. When this happened, no one told the holders of a dozen maps to the treasure.

"Why did you come this way?" Slocum asked. "What did you find in the fort to tell you this was the way to come?"

"The map—" Evangeline started. She bit off the lie. Slocum knew she had only half the map. If she needed to put it together with the half her brother had, she wouldn't know what direction to head. She took a deep breath and said, "I read the commander's logbook. He ordered William out in this direction to hunt for the Cheyenne and try to capture them."

"What happened to the others at the post?"

"Those pages were missing. They'd been torn out. William was sent out on patrol almost three weeks ago."

"It's not unusual for a cavalry company to be in the field that long," Slocum said. It often required a week or more of riding just to reach the trouble spot. In these barren mountains, it might take even longer for a company to ride far enough to matter.

"William came this way, and I thought I could try to track him. I wasn't doing a good job. It's been too long."

Slocum sat down with a tree at his back and watched the water rippling past. How eager was William Dunbar to see his sister? She had stolen half the map from Quentin Magee. Did the cavalry officer even need her part of the map? Had he already found the treasure and ridden off with it? Slocum doubted there was much in the way of family ties in the Dunbar clan.

"No," she said, as if reading his mind. "William wouldn't do that to me. We are *family*: all we've got is each other. And the way the map was separated, both parts are needed to find the burial site. See?" She fished out the tattered paper from her bodice. She handed the paper to him.

Slocum carefully unfolded the paper and saw that pieces had been cut out. He held it up to the sky and blue patches showed through.

"The pieces were cut out and glued onto another sheet," she said. "William's half has to be placed under this one for all the details to come out. I know directions from the legend at the bottom, but I don't know where the starting point is. That's on his half."

"Clever," Slocum allowed. With the map Evangeline had handed him, he might wander these mountains forever hunting for the gold even if he memorized all the details. It was almost better not to even try to use the map, if he wanted to search on his own.

"What are we going to do?" she asked. She took a deep

breath and then asked the question really on her mind.
"What are *you* going to do?"

Slocum shook his head and answered, "I don't rightly
know. But when I figure it out, I'll be sure to let you know."
He tipped his hat forward and settled down for a much
needed sleep. He hoped something might come to him in
his dreams, but he wasn't counting on it.

13

"John?" Evangeline's voice came as a soft breeze, caressing his mind and making him stir slightly. "I hear something. I—it might be the Cheyenne."

He came bolt upright, hand going for his Colt Navy. Evangeline stood near the sluggish stream, a worried look on her face. She pointed up the canyon. For a moment, Slocum heard nothing. Then he made out the faint pounding of horses' hooves. He levered himself to his feet and grabbed the desert bag, slinging it over his shoulder.

"Let's go," he said. "I don't know who it is, but there's a hell of a lot of them. No matter what, I don't want them to find us." The only groups with that many riders were the Cheyenne and Quentin Magee. Either way, Slocum wanted to make himself scarce.

"Where do we go?" Evangeline looked around. There weren't many likely looking places for the pair of them to hide.

"Up the canyon," Slocum decided. It wasn't the best solution but it was quick. Whoever came toward them rode from the northwest. That puzzled him, but the canyons twisted and turned and he didn't have a good map of the area. Magee might have circled about to come at them from a different direction, but Slocum doubted it. That left the Indians.

"We can't outrun them," Evangeline said. "Listen! They're galloping!"

"They'll kill their damn horses if they do that for long. Something's spooked them. When they get it out of their systems, they'll settle down to a more leisurely pace." Even as he spoke, he was swinging up into the saddle. He looked down at the lovely woman.

"John, I—" She looked down at the ground again. "I'm sorry. I shouldn't have left you like I did back at the fort. It was a terrible thing to do."

"We're even. You saved my hide back in San Francisco. This erases any obligation I have."

"No," she protested.

"Get mounted. We've got to keep ahead of them." Slocum didn't wait to see if she followed. He'd said his piece. He meant everything he'd said about the slate being clean. Returning to San Francisco might be dangerous for him if the ring she had given as collateral was phony—and he didn't have any reason to doubt her on this. Still, he had been able to leave that city without having a bullet ripping through his back. That most of what Evangeline had told him was a bald-faced lie irritated the hell out of him.

Some of the gold, if there was any, would go a long way toward putting right that affront. But first they had to stay alive.

He urged his horse up a shale slope to a small plateau. It wasn't much in the way of cover but it got him off the valley floor and put him up where he could see more of what was going on. The riders weren't visible yet, but they would be soon. They weren't letting any moss grow under their feet.

"John, wait for me. Don't leave me. Please!" Evangeline struggled with her horse up the slope. Slocum didn't have any intention of abandoning her. There wasn't anywhere he could go from this small, level area. To continue up the mountain was out of the question. He could only go back down into the canyon.

"I see them," he said, squinting into the sun. He had slept later than he'd thought. The sun was setting over the jagged line of the mountains, making it difficult to see.

Evangeline Dunbar got to the level spot and jumped from her horse. The grateful animal shivered all over. Its sides were lathered and it needed a rest. Slocum hoped the horse would get the chance. If it had to run now, it would collapse within a mile.

"Who are they? Cheyenne?"

"I don't think so," he said. His keen eyes followed a small dust cloud toward the spot where he had come down the mountainside on the far side of the canyon. The trail there was worn as if it was occasionally traveled.

"That's sunlight shining off brass!" exclaimed Evangeline. "That's a cavalry troop!"

Slocum had to agree. He had been a sniper during the war and had gotten to be expert at sighting Union officers. He now saw braid and brass and the blue wool uniforms of enlisted men.

"It might be William's patrol. We've got to go see." Evangeline started to mount again. Slocum grabbed her arm and stopped her.

"Not so fast," he said. "We don't know if they came from Fort Desolation or not. It might be your brother's company. This is about the right time for him to be returning if he'd been sent out on a three week or month circuit of the countryside."

"Then—"

"It might not be him. What do we say if we waltz on up and it's someone else?"

"We'll think of something. John, I've got to know what happened to him. He's my brother."

"And he's got the other half of the map," Slocum finished for her.

"Yes," she said, fire burning in her eyes, "that's right. I will not be cheated out of my fair share. Quentin tried it and failed. It won't happen again."

"You forget. Magee's still at the fort. We'd have to let the cavalry decide between him and us."

"William's my brother. That will count more than anything Quentin might say or do."

Slocum snorted in contempt. Magee was well heeled. Pay was notoriously bad at the frontier outposts. A major or colonel could be bribed for a hundred dollars. An entire company could be bought for less than that. A man with a couple of bottles of whiskey could get anything he wanted.

"Let's follow at a distance. That way, there won't be any nasty surprises."

"Very well," Evangeline said with ill grace. She was champing at the bit to go after the cavalry column. If nothing else, Slocum decided, the woman's horse needed a rest. The air turned cold when the sun finally slid behind the mountains. Only then did Slocum allow Evangeline to start down the treacherous loose shale slope. The twilight made travel risky, and by the time the last of the daylight had faded, Evangeline was ready to quit for the night.

"You did this on purpose," she accused.

"I'm not saying I didn't," Slocum said, "but you'll end up agreeing this is for the best. If that was your brother, another few hours won't much matter."

"But it'll be dawn before we can travel!"

"And well nigh noon before we get back to the fort," he went on. "But the cavalry isn't going to travel much longer in the dark. There's too much chance of a horse stepping into a gopher hole and breaking a leg or losing balance and throwing its rider. They'll bivouac for the night, then go on. We'll be right behind them.''

Slocum intended to watch the cavalry column's approach to the fort, if at all possible. He wanted to see what reception they got—and gave—when Quentin Magee spotted them.

He wondered how Evangeline would want to spend the night. When she pulled her blanket tightly around her body and turned her face away from him, he got his answer. It was about as he expected. Her reaction made it easier for Slocum to get a good night's sleep. He had the feeling that he was going to need to be rested come noon tomorrow.

"I'm tired, John," she complained. "You've pushed us all morning long. We can't overtake the soldiers.''

"I know," he said. They had found the cavalry's camp around ten o'clock. Everything pointed to the blue coats having been gone for over three hours. Slocum knew they couldn't close the gap much on the cavalry column, but he wasn't all that interested in overtaking them. He just wanted to be in the high pass to the north of Fort Desolation to watch what happened when the soldiers rode into their fort.

"Can't we rest?"

"Soon," he promised. He tried to estimate how near they were to the point overlooking the fort. It wasn't more than forty-five minutes' ride away.

Slocum smiled to himself when it took only a half hour to reach the vantage point he wanted. Astride his horse, he was able to look down the winding road leading to the rear of the fort.

"At last," Evangeline said, seeing they had almost reached the end of their journey. "We can see the fort."

"Stay put for a few minutes," Slocum ordered. "The horses can use the rest, and you said you could, too."

"That was hours ago," Evangeline said, completely mis-judging the time. "I've caught my second wind."

"Then you'll be all ready for the fight."

"Fight? What fight?" Evangeline stood in her stirrups

and stared at Fort Desolation. A small gasp escaped her lips
when she saw what was happening below.

Magee's men had opened the fort's front gates. The cavalry column rode up and found itself flanked by the Cheyenne braves. Rifles echoed and arrows whistled through the
air, slicing through the ranks of the hapless soldiers. They
tried to reach the gates but many were slain. And when the
survivors of the Indian ambush did get to what they thought
was the safety of the fort, Magee's men opened up on them.

The blistering crossfire cut down even more.

"They're being slaughtered. My brother's going to get
killed! John, we've got to do something."

"What do you suggest?" He watched as the Indians
stormed the fort. Blood lust had wiped out their fear of the
crazy man inside. Slocum chewed on his lower lip as he
watched the three factions melt together. Magee's men began firing into both Cheyenne and cavalry ranks. The three-
way battle swirled like the ocean's surf, ebbing and flowing.
The final tidal thrust was into Fort Desolation.

"The Indians have gone inside the fort," Slocum said.
"That would usually be suicidal. Soldiers on the walls
would cut them down where they stood. But not now."

The soldiers had abandoned their fort. There was no sup-
porting fire for the handful of troopers still fighting. As
Slocum watched, some silent alliance was formed. Magee
and his men came to the realization that they stood a better
chance if they threw in with the soldiers. But by the time
this uneasy coalition had formed, it was almost too late.

"We've got to go to them. We can help. An extra pair
of guns—"

"Two more guns in that won't mean shit," Slocum said
brutally. "The Cheyenne have them boxed up now. The
fort's not protecting them, it's guaranteeing they'll be cut
down."

"We can do something."

Slocum held back until he saw an officer forming the
ragged remains of his command for a thrust back out of the

fort. He had to ride past a gauntlet of Cheyenne, but it was the only way he could escape certain death. His post was in enemy hands. He had to try for freedom outside Fort Desolation.

"Him," Slocum said. "We'll try to help *him*."

Evangeline wanted to race headlong into battle. He managed to keep her pace a more sedate trot. As it was, their horses were lathered and gasping by the time they reached the rear wall of the fort. Slocum drew his rifle from its scabbard and levered a round into the chamber. He looked and saw that Evangeline had found a military carbine somewhere and had taken it from the fort.

"Let's try not to get killed," Slocum said.

"That's my brother. I know it," she said with grim determination. "I'll rescue him."

"Just don't be taken alive by the Indians," Slocum warned. Then he urged his horse forward. As he passed the corner of the fort, he saw that four troopers were less than a hundred yards distant, huddled behind their dead horses. They were giving a good accounting of themselves. A half dozen fallen Cheyenne braves showed the excellence of the soldiers' marksmanship.

As Slocum rode closer, he knew it might have also been desperation that made the soldiers fight so. They were going to die. The Indians outnumbered them a dozen to one. Where the Cheyenne had gotten the additional warriors, he didn't know. It was apparent they had a small army fighting and no single cavalry column was a match for them.

"They've seen us," Evangeline called. "They're coming for us, John!"

He didn't need to be told. He was already swinging his rifle around and firing. He got off three quick shots that did nothing. The fourth slug ripped through a war lance and jerked it from the brave's hand. His fifth shot took the brave from his horse.

But there were three Indians to take that one's place. Slocum had never seen so many Cheyenne in his life. If he had known there was this kind of battle going on, he would never have ridden into the middle of it. All he could do now was throw in with the soldiers hunkered down behind their dead horses and pray for a miracle.

Even before he had hit the ground running to join the soldiers, the miracle happened. An inhuman shriek cut through the din of battle—and it didn't stop. It rose until Slocum wanted to cry out in pain. Then the shriek turned into wild animal howling.

Sergeant Ben Madsen was somewhere nearby.

The Cheyenne heard the demented sergeant's caterwauling and melted away as if by magic. Slocum fired a few times in the direction of the retreating Cheyenne just to vent some of his anger and frustration at being caught in this fight.

"Damn, mister, are we glad to see you," said a bloodied trooper. "Whoever you got making all that noise sure turned the trick."

Slocum didn't get a chance to correct the soldier's mistaken idea. A bullet came ripping from the direction of the fort and caught him squarely in the back of the head. The soldier jerked forward and fell over a dead horse, his arms outstretched.

Slocum dived for cover but couldn't spot the rifleman who had taken the soldier's life just when he had thought he was safe.

Behind him he heard Evangeline crying.

He turned and saw her cradling a man in her arms. Slocum didn't have to be told this was William Dunbar. And he didn't have to examine him to know the man didn't have long to live, not with a pair of Cheyenne arrows stuck in his chest.

14

The Cheyenne had taken to their heels and were riding off in a huge dust cloud. The troopers who were still alive wandered about in a daze, looking for leadership—and the only surviving officer was William Dunbar. From the way the arrows jutted from his chest Slocum knew the man wasn't long for this world.

"Will, oh, Will, don't die on me." Evangeline held his head in her arms. Trickles of blood oozed from the corners of his mouth, but it was the pink froth that came from his nose that told Slocum William Dunbar was a dead man. An arrow had pierced the man's lungs, and he was drowning in his own blood.

"Evie, you came," the dying officer said. He reached up and touched her cheek. Slocum watched. He frowned when he saw the gold wedding ring on the man's hand. Evangeline hadn't said anything about her brother being married.

"We've got to get out of here," Slocum said, kneeling beside the two. "Magee's inside the fort. I don't think his men took all that many casualties. It was your column that got chewed up, lieutenant."

"Quentin's here?" Dunbar's eyes snapped into sharp focus as anger flooded him. "I ought to have known. That—"

"Will, don't. We'll get you out of here. This is John Slocum. He's been helping me."

Dunbar took Evangeline's hand and held it up. For the first time Slocum noticed the small white band on the woman's ring finger. Dunbar sought the ring that ought to have been there and wasn't.

"Evie?"

"She sold the ring to pay for the railroad tickets to reach you," Slocum lied. "Seeing you meant that much to her."

"I love you, Evie."

"Will, please hold on. We've got to get away. We can go somewhere and you—"

Slocum shook her shoulder. She tried to pull away. She knew Dunbar was dying and refused to admit it. Slocum knew she wouldn't ask what had to be asked, so he took the bull by the horns and said, "We need the map. We don't want Magee to get your half."

"You have his part of the map?" Dunbar's voice came out weak and quavering. The pink froth gushed from his mouth. He had only a few more minutes left before he died.

"Yes, Will. Here. See?" Evangeline held up the map.

"In my pocket. Get my half of the map. Find the gold. Evie, live a good life. I love you."

Those were William Dunbar's last words. He sagged in the woman's arms. She lowered him to the dusty ground and simply stared.

"Get the map, Evangeline," Slocum urged. "Magee's men are coming out to see what the hell happened. They won't be able to miss us."

She fished around under Dunbar's uniform jacket and then

tugged. The map had been pinned to his chest by an arrow and then blood had soaked it. Forcing back tears, she pulled the map free.

"Let's go." Slocum looked nervously toward Fort Desolation. Magee rode out on his horse looking for all the world like a conquering hero. He had even taken the time to wax his mustache.

"John," she said, looking at him with tear-filled eyes, "how long have you known?"

"That Dunbar was your husband? Just seeing you together told me."

"That was my wedding ring I gave those three gamblers back at the Union Club," she said. "I needed your help and that was the only way I could get it."

"Come on," Slocum said. Magee had spotted them. He forced her to climb onto a trooper's horse. He vaulted into the saddle of his own and put the spurs to the animal's flanks. Slocum wasn't sure if Magee would give chase. He thought the man would.

Slocum wanted to be ready with an ambush that would take Quentin Magee out of action. Without him, the rest of his men might give up the hunt. They knew they were looking for treasure but Magee might not have given them the complete story.

"Over there," Slocum said, pointing. "We can take positions behind the boulders and pick Magee off when he comes around the bend in the road."

"What about the Cheyenne?" asked Evangeline. "Won't the gunfire bring them back?"

"I don't think so. The way they took off when Madsen began his caterwauling tells me they've given up on Fort Desolation. They might not stop running until they reach the Tongue River."

"I don't want to kill Quentin," she said suddenly.

"He'll kill you." Slocum looked at her. The woman's tears were dried and a set to her chin told him she wasn't going to argue. He realized then that Magee wouldn't harm her.

"There's more that I haven't told you, John. Will and I were married, but he was in the Army and it was so far out here—"

"And a woman gets lonely. So you and Magee sort of set up house back in San Francisco."

"That's a crude way of putting it," she said primly, "but it is essentially correct. I have nothing against Quentin. He's really a dear, dear man."

"He's a dear man who'd hang my scalp out to dry," Slocum snapped. "He may still love you but he's got nothing but blood in his eye for me." Slocum wondered anew what he had gotten himself into. Marital infidelity didn't trouble him much. He and Evangeline had enjoyed one another's company. He might not have been much interested in pushing her for sexual favors if she'd said she was married, but she had never given him any hint until the fight back at the fort.

That was her choice. That he wasn't the only one enjoying her charms didn't much bother him, either. It did rankle that Quentin Magee was likely to torture him before he killed him, though. And the reasons had little to do with the treasure map. Magee looked to be the kind of man who took things personally.

"Did Magee know you and Dunbar were married?"

When Evangeline didn't answer, Slocum knew the woman had spent much of her life lying about herself and her intentions.

"Give me the map you took from your bro—" He stopped and corrected himself. "The map you got from your husband. Hand it over."

"But John, we're in this together. We—"

"Now!"

She silently handed him the blood-soaked paper. Slocum carefully opened it and pressed it flat against a rock. He occasionally looked down the road to see if Magee was coming. When he saw and heard nothing, he went back to carefully spreading out the flimsy sheet. It took him a few seconds to understand what he had.

"This isn't the other half of the map."

"What? That can't be. Will said—" Evangeline pushed him aside and stared at the bloody paper. Evangeline's mouth dropped open. "He couldn't do this to me. He wouldn't!"

Slocum looked over her shoulder and carefully began reading what he could of the words not blotted out by William Dunbar's blood. A few parts of the map were missing because of the arrow that had ripped through the paper before taking the man's life. But Slocum figured out what they really had.

"This is a map to where he hid the real map," he said. "He must not have wanted to take his half out on patrol."

"That makes sense. If anything happened to him and he had the other half, it would be lost. By leaving it inside the fort, it would be safe. Where does this take us?"

Slocum heard how Evangeline was once more using the word "we" when she talked about finding the treasure. He wondered how long that would last if he recovered the missing portion of the map.

"It looks as if he put the map in a coffee can. Some of the instructions are missing." Slocum rubbed his hand against his trousers to get rid of some of the still sticky blood. "The one thing that is real clear, though, is that William's half is *inside* Fort Desolation."

"Quentin's still in the fort. How are we ever going to search for the rest of the map?"

"There's got to be a way. It doesn't look as if Magee's coming after us. He must not have wanted to tangle with the Cheyenne braves." Slocum hardly had the words out of his mouth when he heard the soft scuffing of leather on stone. He shoved Evangeline hard, ducked, and swung around, his hand flashing toward the knife sheathed at the small of his back.

Powerful fingers closed on his wrist. Slocum was slammed back against the rock where the bloody map lay. The breath was almost knocked from his lungs by the impact. His right hand was forced open by the steel grip the Cheyenne brave had on him.

As suddenly as the Indian had attacked, he stopped. Slocum shoved him away, not sure what had happened.

The knife in the middle of the brave's back told the story. When he had dropped his knife, Evangeline had picked it up and used it.

"John, there might be others."

"My thoughts exactly," he said, yanking the knife from the Cheyenne warrior's back. "He got careless or I'd've never heard him." His green eyes worked up the slope looking for traces of other Indians. The one lying dead at his feet was the only one he saw.

"We'd better go. The Cheyenne might be coming back. What keeps them here?"

"I wish I knew," Slocum said. For a tribe newly escaped from their Oklahoma reservation, they had no reason to stick like glue to Fort Desolation. He didn't think this was their ancestral land. All that he had heard mentioned their exodus to Montana. Slocum just wished to hell they had gone on through and not stayed.

"They get spooked whenever they hear Sergeant Madsen howling, but they never go far," Evangeline complained. She stared at the dead brave and shuddered. "I don't like the feeling when I killed him."

"You had to kill him. It was him or me," Slocum said. He was damned glad she had chosen the way she did.

"You don't understand," she said. "I *enjoyed* it. I wanted to kill him. He might have been the one who killed William."

"He probably wasn't," Slocum said. He hoped Evangeline didn't get into the habit of killing. Sooner or later he was going to have to turn his back on her. When he did, he didn't like the notion she'd stab him, too.

They led their horses down to the road. Slocum looked around but saw no sign of either Magee's men or the Cheyenne war party. The brave Evangeline had killed was probably a lone scout sent out by the main party. If so, when he didn't return, there would be others dispatched to look for him.

Slocum hoped finding the other half of the map was worth all the bloodshed and trouble.

"We can sneak back into the fort," Evangeline said. "We can get in and find where Will hid his part of the map. Then we can get the Spaniards' treasure and clear out of here. I've taken a distinct disliking to Desolation Point, Utah."

He silently agreed with her. But what were they going to do after they found the hidden gold? Was she considering an equal split? Slocum was a newcomer to the hunt. Evangeline might decide she'd get better treatment if she threw in with Quentin Magee. After all, the two of them had been lovers.

Slocum found himself studying Evangeline Dunbar and desiring her. She was a lovely woman. Even after the fighting, the blood and dust, the horror of killing, she was attractive. Her long brunette hair blew back in the gentle wind like a banner. She sat straight and proud on her horse and the sight of her long, slender legs turned Slocum's mouth dry. In spite of everything, he desired her.

"There's a way into the fort I found after you left," she said.

Even her voice appealed to him. Soft, melodic, a lover's caress. And she had just killed. She had betrayed her husband and lover and she would betray him, given the chance.

"What?" Slocum shook himself. "Sorry. I was busy thinking about other things." The way she looked at him made him angry. A tiny smile crept to the corners of Evangeline's mouth. It was as if she had heard his thoughts and knew what he wanted—and she was telling him with the smile that she wanted the same thing.

He damned himself for a fool, but it did no good.

"There're a few loose timbers at the rear of the fort. I found them just after you left. I was afraid the Cheyenne might be able to get into the fort that way. We can pry the saplings apart and slip inside. We can get the map and be out of there before Quentin even realizes anyone's sneaked into the fort."

"That's a better plan than just riding up or waiting for Magee to leave. He might decide he likes the fort and stay for weeks."

"Quentin is a stubborn man. He never gives up. I'm afraid that we might have to kill him."

Slocum said nothing. Evangeline had tasted killing and liked the power it gave her. That wasn't good.

"We can camp a few hundred yards toward the wooded area until dark. Then we can find these loose saplings of yours and finish the job."

"We might be able to find a way to make the time pass faster," she said, slowly licking her lips in an obvious invitation.

"There's no time. The sun's getting ready to go down in less than twenty minutes," Slocum said. "Besides, the Cheyenne are prowling around here. I don't want to get, uh, occupied and have one of them lift my scalp."

"But what a way to go," Evangeline teased. She turned and used her reins to whip her horse to a faster pace. Slocum was hard pressed to keep up with her. They found a spot near the creek and watered their horses. Slocum made sure their tethers were tight before he motioned to the woman to join him. Twilight settled like a gray veil and cloaked their quick dash to the rear wall of the fort.

"Where is the spot you found?"

Evangeline signaled him to follow. He stayed a few paces behind, aware of the sentries on the wall above. She found the loose saplings in the wall and began tugging at them. The creaking and groaning noise sounded like cannon fire to Slocum. He paused for a moment to see if the guards

Magee had posted were going to investigate. When he saw that they were moving along the walkway in the other direction, he added his efforts to Evangeline's. In less than five minutes they had a space large enough for them both to squeeze through.

"There is William's starting point," Evangeline said. She pointed to the flagpole.

"We can't go there and pace off the distances," Slocum said. "Magee's got men moving all around. I'm not sure if they are patrolling or if they're just nervous after what happened today."

It didn't much matter the reason for the men's uneasiness. Slocum watched as Magee's foreman mustered his men and sent them on meaningless excursions around the fort. No matter how many men he occupied this way, though, he always had three posted on the walls as lookouts.

"I can guess where Will might have gone after twenty paces," Evangeline said. "He had long legs. That would have taken him to the corner of the armory."

"From there he turned north and went ten paces," Slocum said, reciting the instructions from memory. It was hard to see where this would take them. The falling darkness turned the inside of the fort into a pitch-black box.

"After the ten paces," Evangeline went on, "you're supposed to turn east, then come in this direction until— what? I don't remember that part."

"Until the edges of the buildings are lined up. Then the map is in a coffee can. The part where it was hidden was destroyed."

"That doesn't matter," Evangeline said, her excitement mounting. "Look. Follow the route. That spot by the edge of the barracks is about where the edge of the commander's quarters and the adjutant's office would line up. Turn around and go straight along that path and you'd end up back by the outhouses. William must have hidden the map there!"

"I only know one way to find out." Slocum edged along the wall, then boldly walked out toward the outhouses. If anyone saw him, the shadows would hide his features. If the sentries saw a man sneaking in this direction, they'd be sure to raise a ruckus. It was safer to be daring now than cautious.

Evangeline followed him to the long wood shack set near the back wall of the fort. She dropped to her knees and began digging.

"What are you doing?" he asked.

"Looking for the map. What do you think?"

"I think your brother wouldn't have buried it. Not here. The ground's too soft."

"But—"

Slocum edged around the small wood building, studying the walls. He stopped when he saw gouge marks on the back. Weather had discolored the spots where splinters had been pulled free. He reckoned the discoloration of the underlying wood was about right for a month or more in this dry climate.

"Up," Slocum said. "That's where the map is. He put it on the roof of the outhouse."

He put his boot into a convenient knothole, then launched himself upward. His other foot banged against the wood about where he had seen the splinters. William Dunbar must have been about the same height as he was. Slocum got his elbows over the edge of the low sloping roof and looked around. The crude wood shingles seemed to offer no hiding place for anything as large as an empty coffee can.

He was just about ready to give up in disgust when he saw it. One shingle among the dry, rotting wood was shiny. He grabbed at it. The flattened coffee can came free easily. Slocum dropped back to the ground with it clutched in his hand.

"The map! At last," cried Evangeline.

Slocum pried open the coffee can and found a small slip of paper.

"Give me that," she said, yanking it from his hand. The

woman's face fell when she saw that the paper scrap was blank.

"It's only the corner of a bigger sheet," Slocum said. "It tore off when someone removed the map."

They had risked everything to reenter Fort Desolation and had come up empty-handed.

15

"He cheated me. He stole it!" Evangeline Dunbar was beside herself with rage. Her hands shook and tears of frustration ran down her cheeks, leaving dusty trails. She held the flattened coffee can as if it were a rattlesnake with six-inch-long fangs. She started to throw it away when Slocum grabbed it from her.

"Who are you talking about?" Slocum said. He crouched down behind the outhouse, his mind racing. Something wasn't right but he couldn't put his finger on it.

"Quentin. He got to the map first. And now he's going to beat us to the gold!"

"He still doesn't have the half you stole from him," Slocum pointed out.

"That might not matter. He's sharp. He might be able to remember every detail. You shouldn't underestimate him."

"And you shouldn't overestimate him," Slocum said.

"Why's he still inside the fort if he knows where the gold is?"

"He might have just found the map. He's waiting for dawn before he rides out to get it." Evangeline's breathing increased. She almost panted now and a fiery light came to her brown eyes. "That's it! We'll follow the son of a bitch and steal the treasure from him when he retrieves it. That'll show him!"

"He's still got eight or ten men," Slocum said. "Getting it away from that many men isn't going to be easy."

"We can do it. We must. For William, we must."

"Magee doesn't have the map," Slocum said. He followed this basic idea to its logical conclusion. Magee was still in Fort Desolation. There was no reason to stay here if he had the map—and he certainly wasn't going to stay if the Cheyenne war party kept returning.

"But he must. Who else would take it?"

"He hadn't found it before the cavalry patrol returned," Slocum said. "Magee would have been long gone. He knows the Cheyenne are out there. He's no fool. Nobody's able to fight off that many braves. And there hasn't been time for him to find it since the attack that killed your husband."

"But who's got it?"

An inhuman howling echoed through the fort. Slocum turned to find the source. It was difficult locating Ben Madsen because of the way the undulating sound seemed to change position constantly. The walls of the fort and the distant rocky cliffs played tricks with the rising and falling sound.

"Him? He's got it? That doesn't make any sense, John."

"It makes more sense than believing Magee's got the other half of the map. Madsen's somewhere inside the fort. It's hard to tell but I think he's in that direction. You've scouted the fort better than I have. What's over there?"

"Nothing," Evangeline said. "Just a pile of garbage. It

was next to a small garden. They must have thought to make a compost heap."

"Perfect," Slocum said. "Where else would a crazy man like Madsen hide but under a pile of garbage?"

"That's silly," Evangeline said. "Quentin's got the map. He must!"

Slocum didn't bother listening to her plea to gun down Quentin and recover the map. Everything he had thought about the San Francisco dandy had to be right. The times were wrong for Magee to have found the map after the Cheyenne attack, and he wasn't the type to waste time if he had the map in his possession. The only thing that might have held him at the fort if he did have William Dunbar's half was to set a trap for Evangeline. He might actually need her half of the map to find the gold.

His head began to hurt with all the possibilities. His father had told him a long time back to keep it simple and not try to switch teams in the middle of a bog. If an idea covered all the possible endings, then the straightest road to it was the best.

"John, you're not listening."

"Hush up or Magee's men will hear you." Slocum looked to the sentries still pacing along the walls. Their complete attention was directed outward toward the Indian threat. He didn't want to draw unwanted attention to himself. He was a sitting duck as long as he was inside the fort.

He smelled the compost heap before he saw it. He went straight to it, hand resting on the ebony handle of his Colt Navy. Madsen hadn't seemed dangerous but being crazy might only be a role he played. If he had the map and was looking for the other half, that meant he was saner than Slocum had thought.

"John, it's terrible here. I can hardly stand the stench." Evangeline held her nose and turned away. Slocum ignored the odor and began poking through the decaying garbage. It would have made good fertilizer had any of the troopers remained behind to use it on their small garden.

When Slocum's poking revealed a wood door, he stopped and began scooping up the garbage and throwing it to one side. A few minutes of the odious work revealed Madsen's hiding place. The man had put a small crate down and heaped the garbage over it. Then he had dug down into the ground and made a spot large enough to sleep in.

"You were right. Madsen *lives* here," Evangeline said in amazement.

"If you can call it living. There's no telling where he is right now." Slocum went to the fort wall and knelt down, his six-shooter drawn. If necessary, he was willing to wait all night for the madman to return to his hidey hole.

"I'll check to see if the map's inside." Before he could stop her, Evangeline wiggled down into the hole. She returned a few minutes later, covered with garbage and looking disgusted.

"You didn't find it," Slocum said. "He wouldn't leave it here. If he is as mobile as he seems, he'd keep it with him." He remembered locking Madsen in the fort's jail. If he had searched him then, he would have found the map. Slocum smiled ruefully. Back then he didn't know he was looking for a map.

Not for the first time Slocum wondered if this was worth the promise of phantom gold. There were so many Lost Dutchman Mines, so many legends and rumors and outright lies told over a bottle of whiskey, that he might be chasing his own tail.

He started to speak to Evangeline, to tell her he was leaving, when he saw a shadow moving across another shadow. The slight difference in darkness warned him that Madsen was getting close. His sense of smell had long since been overwhelmed by the garbage heap, but his eyesight was as keen as ever.

He motioned her to silence and pointed. He felt her stiffen, a thoroughbred racehorse waiting for the big competition. He lifted his six-shooter and aimed carefully. If

Madsen came at them, Slocum was going to be ready for
the madman.

The pistol wasn't needed. Madsen passed within a few
feet of where they stood in the darkness and never saw
them. When the crazy sergeant had passed by and gone on
a few more feet, Slocum swung his gun. The barrel con-
nected with the side of Madsen's head. The dull crunch
sounded like a gunshot, but the way Madsen fell facedown
in the dust told Slocum he had done the right thing. He
looked up to see if one of Magee's sentries had heard the
sound. There wasn't any hint that the impact of metal against
skull had caused any interest.

Slocum dragged Madsen back into shadows. The moon
would be up in a another ten minutes. Even though it was
waning, it would still cast a silvery light almost like day.
Slocum wanted to get the map from the sergeant and be out
of Fort Desolation by then.

He cocked the pistol and shoved it into Madsen's mouth.
"Do as you're told and I won't pull the trigger." The man
may have been crazy but he wasn't stupid. He saw death
written on Slocum's face.

"John, do you have to do it this way?"

"Quiet," Slocum ordered sharply. He wished Evangeline
would let him get on with this in his own way. There wasn't
time to coax the map from Madsen's clutches.

Ben Madsen gurgled around the barrel and began to
squirm as his senses returned. Slocum pulled the gun out
just a little to allow the man to speak without choking.

"You understand me? You answer honestly and I won't
pull the trigger."

"Unnerstan," Madsen choked out.

"Where's the map Lieutenant Dunbar hid?"

"Dunno." Madsen almost choked when Slocum jammed
the barrel a couple inches back into his mouth.

"You're lying. The map was in a coffee can on top of
the outhouse. You took it. You've been hanging around to
get the other half of the map. Maybe you thought Magee

had it and you could join forces. That doesn't matter. We want the map.''

"Doan haffit."

"He's lying, John. He *must* have it."

"I'm inclined to agree with the lady. Is it worth your life?"

"Don't have it," Madsen said more clearly when Slocum withdrew the gun from the man's mouth. "Honest!"

"Why are you still in Fort Desolation?"

"I'm crazy! I like howling at the moon. I can't help myself." Madsen started to let out another of his inhuman cries. Slocum hit him on the side of the head with his left fist. The blow caused Madsen to moan rather than howl like a dog.

"The map. You give it to us and you can go bay at the moon like a coyote all you want."

"They got it. That's why they all left. I didn't know what it was."

"Who are you talking about?" demanded Evangeline.

"The soldiers. A couple dozen left two weeks back. They found something and they all left. Then the Indians attacked and killed the ones who were left."

"You're lying. There wasn't any trace of bodies when we rode into the fort," Slocum said.

"The Indians took 'em out. I don't know why. This must be some sort of burial ground, holy land or something."

"That would explain why they keep returning," Slocum said, "in spite of your howls."

"I like it," Madsen confided. "I like watching them turn tail and run when I bellow."

"The soldiers might be ahead of us. Twenty or thirty of them," said Slocum. "Is it worth continuing?"

"Yes!" Evangeline Dunbar was adamant on this. "That's my gold—*our* gold."

Slocum worried over the options open to him. Going up against that many soldiers bent on retrieving a hoard of gold didn't set well with him. Greed had driven them to desert their post. They might have killed their officers—or the officers might have led the men off to get the golden Spanish treasure. No matter what had happened, the soldiers had left their command unlawfully and weren't likely to greet anyone on their trail with open arms.

Even as this crossed Slocum's mind, other, smaller items began to intrude. Details didn't mesh.

"You said smallpox had wiped out the garrison," he said to Madsen. "Why'd you lie? Why not just tell us the troopers had gone off on a treasure hunt?"

The man's eyes darted around like those of a trapped animal. Madsen wanted to escape. Slocum shoved his pistol into the man's gut and said, "If I fired my six-shooter right now, there wouldn't be much sound. Your belly would suck up all the noise. And I'll pull the trigger unless you start telling the truth."

"John, he may not know what the truth is."

Slocum had to admit the woman might have a point. Sergeant Ben Madsen was as likely to lie as not when he opened his mouth. This got Slocum to thinking along other lines.

"Why didn't you join the soldiers going off to get the gold?"

"Don't need gold," Madsen grunted.

The truth hit Slocum like a blow to the gut. He stepped back and stared at the supine man and shook his head.

"What's the matter, John?" Evangeline sounded anxious.

"We're getting out of here. Everything he's said is a damned lie. You were right. He can't tell the difference between the truth and what's boiling up in his fevered brain."

"What do you mean?"

"He's not a sergeant in the cavalry. Hell, I doubt if he s even a soldier. Is that right, Madsen?"

"Not a horse soldier," Madsen said, cowering away. "Hate the horse soldiers. They're always mean to me."

Slocum motioned toward the wall and the opening. He wanted to get away from Fort Desolation and find a quiet spot where he could think things through. They weren't going to get the other half of the map. He wasn't even sure they'd ever find out what happened to the Fort Desolation garrison.

But there still might be a chance at getting the gold.

16

The demented howls followed John Slocum from Fort Desolation. He wanted to clap both hands over his ears to shut out Ben Madsen's cries but refrained. It was better to get out of earshot than to temporarily stop the way the shrieks drove straight for the center of his brain and then dug around until he was quivering.

"Are you all right, John?" Evangeline asked. "You don't look too good."

"I'm fine," he lied. "I just need some time to get everything squared away in my head. There's too many loose ends dangling for my liking."

"We didn't get the map." Evangeline sounded more dejected than he felt. "I suppose we ought to give up on the search and return to San Francisco." As she thought about this, she shook her head slowly. "No, not San Francisco. There is too much chance we might run into Quentin or someone who works for him. He isn't going

to stay here much longer if he can't find either the map
or us."

They reached their horses. Slocum mounted and rode
slowly back toward the pass to the north. Something about
it drew him. If he were drawing a map, that's the vantage
point he would use as a starting point. The pass was higher
than the fort and the valley surrounding it and it gave a
good view in both directions. The rocky canyon beyond
wandered around but afforded a pathway deeper into the
mountains.

"What is it?" Evangeline asked.

"I was just thinking about what the other half of the map
might have on it."

"A starting point," Evangeline said bitterly. "Without
knowing where to begin, what good is the map we have?"

"We've got to think that the Indians hiding the gold
used natural markers, ones not likely to change over the
years."

"Great," Evangeline said in disgust. "They might use
shadows at times of year, mountain peaks, or just about
anything. They might have even used lightning struck trees
that don't exist anymore or bleached out steers' skulls by
the side of some forgotten road. We'll never find the
gold!"

"The pass leads to the north," Slocum said. "The
Cheyenne homelands are to the north. It seems a good
place to consider a starting point. Your brother went out
on patrol in that general direction—and he didn't take the
map."

"That might mean he wasn't going in the right direction."

"Or it might mean he had memorized the map and wa
getting the lay of the land, just waiting for your half t
complete the search."

"William might have left rock markers," Evangelin
said, warming to the notion. "He might have done all th
surveying needed to get us started!"

She fell silent for a few minutes as joy replaced her doubts. Then she asked, "What about the soldiers who took the map? We're likely to run into them, aren't we?"

"Maybe not. There's not a great deal Ben Madsen told us that was true. We might never know why the fort was abandoned the way it was." Slocum snorted and shook his head. "Fort Desolation. It's well named."

"Maybe they were transferred suddenly," suggested Evangeline.

"Not likely. They left their cannon and didn't bother telling your brother and his company. I think there might have been a mass desertion. They saw the Cheyenne coming and hightailed it for parts unknown. Most posts have three or four desertions a month. Fort Desolation just had two years's worth all at once."

Slocum didn't like the sound of it, but it was as probable as any of the other stories he had heard. Maybe there had been a smallpox scare. That would make grown men quake in their boots. The fort was in the middle of nowhere. Who was to go after a trooper who just took off and ran for his life? Or maybe Madsen was right about the soldiers finding the treasure map and going after it. The lure of gold was enough to make most men crazy with greed. Slocum had only himself to look at for a good example of that.

He should have left a long time back. He had stayed to fight Indians and Quentin Magee and madmen and for what? A double-timing, conniving, beautiful woman? That might be part of it, Slocum knew, but he couldn't see that he and Evangeline had much of a future. She was too easy with the truth. In her own way, she was as crazy—and as unpredictable—as Ben Madsen.

But the gold! There might be enough to keep him happy for a long, long time. It was a lousy bet, he knew, but what did he really have to risk finding out? His life was on the line every minute he stayed near Desolation Point, Utah. The Indians and Quentin Magee were both out for his blood.

"What do we look for, John?"

"I'm not really sure," he said, urging his horse back up the slope into the pass. The moon had risen and was already hiding itself behind the mountains. False dawn lit the sky. He hadn't realized they had been so long on the trail. It seemed just a few minutes since they had crept like thieves from Fort Desolation.

"William wouldn't have been blatant about what he did. He had a company of men with him."

"There's a lot to be said for being an officer," Slocum contradicted. "He could do anything he wanted, and all they could do is wonder why he was acting the way he did."

They rode until past noon. Slocum stopped and finished what food they had with them. He needed to hunt to get some fresh game, and Evangeline ought to search out tubers and roots to boil to go with the meat. There were too many things they ought to do and no time to do any of them. Slocum felt the weight of time pressing down on him. It wouldn't be much longer before Magee ventured out from the fort and sought them. They hadn't bothered hiding their trail. The henchmen with Magee would have no trouble locating their prey if they were the least bit trailwise—and Slocum saw no reason to doubt their abilities.

And the Cheyenne were always on his mind. They ran off only to return repeatedly to Fort Desolation. The notion that this was holy ground wouldn't leave Slocum's head. It explained a great deal. The Indians wouldn't want to give up the spirits of their dead with a crazy man hooting and hollering.

They'd be hard-pressed to come right out and kill Ben Madsen, too. The Indians both feared and respected the insane, believing they spoke directly to the gods. Only when Madsen decided to take off and leave on his own would the Cheyenne war party be convinced that they could perform whatever rituals needed doing.

"The cavalry column rode this way," Slocum said,

studying the tracks in the dust. There wasn't much to go on but he found enough piles of horse manure to tell him a sizable number of men had ridden by here within the last few days.

"John, what's that over there?" Evangeline pointed. Slocum's eyes lit up when he saw the two stone cairns built on the small rise. He hurried over and examined them. There wasn't any question these were newly built—maybe about the same time Dunbar's company had come through—and that they were an arrow pointing northward.

"Let's see the map," Slocum said. He waited while Evangeline pulled it out of her bodice. He placed the map atop the first cairn and lined things up.

His heart began to race. He knew how to get to the hidden gold.

Four days of hard travel had taken their toll on Slocum, Evangeline, and their horses. The animals were so tired they staggered as they picked their way along the rocky canyon floor. Slocum had finally insisted that Evangeline get off and walk alongside her horse before it collapsed under her. He had been on the ground almost all day and still his horse was lathered and panting. They couldn't go on much longer without suffering severe exhaustion, yet Slocum had the smell of gold in his nostrils. He knew the treasure trove wasn't far off. The half of the Dunbar map proved it to him.

"I need food, John. It's been forever since I ate."

"I know," he told her, "but we're close. Your map says we're close. Just a few minutes more."

"All the gold in the world won't do either of us any good if we die of starvation."

Slocum said nothing. He kept moving stolidly, putting one foot in front of the other and ignoring her pleas to stop for food. They didn't have that much left. There hadn't been much time for foraging or hunting. When he had seen Quentin Magee's men on their trail three days earlier, he had insisted on traveling as fast as they could. There wasn't any good way to lose the San Francisco dandy in these narrow canyons; all they could hope to do was stay well ahead of him and his henchmen, find the gold, and get the hell out of the Desolation Mountains.

That was easier to plan than to do. Slocum finally knew he had reached the point where he couldn't go on much longer. Evangeline had to be even more tuckered out.

"I'll see to getting us some food," he said. He looked up the high stone walls and tried to estimate the time of day. The sun had already passed the notch above—it was past noon. Pulling his watch from his pocket, he checked and saw that it was almost two o'clock. They had less than two hours of sunlight left. Being in such a deep gorge had its drawbacks. The way the walls cut off the bright spring-time sun was just one of them.

Slocum listened hard for echoes along the canyon and thought he heard strange sounds. He tried to figure out what they were. They came regular and steady like a horse walking, but they were muffled.

"Do you hear that?" he asked.

Evangeline cocked her head to one side and then nodded. "What is it?" she asked.

"Maybe it's the ghost of the Spanish conquistador whose gold got stolen."

"Don't say things like that," she snapped. "It's disrespectful of the dead."

"And stealing their gold isn't?" He listened harder and finally decided that the sound came from ahead of them in the canyon. That was bad news.

"What's the noise?" she asked, ignoring his jibe.

"We've got Indians waiting for us down the canyon," he said. "They've bound their horses' hooves in rawhide to muffle the sound as they cross a rocky stretch." He looked around. The Indians' horses would stay bound up all day in terrain like this. The real question was who the Indians thought they were sneaking up on.

"We're close to where the gold is hidden, aren't we?"

"Reckon so," said Slocum. He worried about being caught between Magee's men following and the Indians ahead. "I'm going to do some scouting. Give me the map, then look around and see if you can't rustle us up something to eat. There's got to be a lizard or two running loose in these rocks."

"Lizards?"

"Or snakes. They make mighty fine eating when your backbone's rubbing up against your belly."

Evangeline looked at him skeptically. She fished out the map and passed it to him without a word. Slocum checked his six-shooter and then started off on foot. He climbed onto a pile of boulders, then made his way slowly upward until he reached the sheer face of the cliff that towered over them. Scaling this was no mean feat, but Slocum only wanted to go up a hundred feet or so to get a good look both ways in the narrow ravine.

What he saw made him smile.

Almost a mile ahead were several small campfires. Smoke rose in lazy swirls and then vanished when the gusty winds whipped down from over the top of the canyon. The Cheyenne had a small camp there, not more than half a dozen warriors from the look of the makeshift corral they'd built from a few fallen limbs and a length of rope. Still, six braves was more than Slocum could hope to fight.

But what made him smile was the sight of Quentin Magee and his men a mile behind. They had made good time keeping up with Slocum and Evangeline. Now it was time for Slocum to end two of his problems at the same time.

Less than a hundred yards from where he and Evangeline had stopped was a narrow canyon leading to the east. Slocum pulled out his map and held it up. Part of the canyon they were in was missing from the map, but not this branch.

The gold was supposed to lie at the end of that small box canyon.

He folded the map and put it back into his pocket and then descended from his aerie. By the time he got back to his small camp, Evangeline was holding two blue-tailed lizards.

"These?" she asked in disgust. "You want us to eat these?"

"I don't know how you caught them," Slocum said. "Usually if you grab them by the tail, it comes off and the lizard gets away."

"I dropped my jacket over them and pinned them to the ground," she said. "We're going to eat them?"

"Not right away. Either let 'em go or kill 'em so we can eat them later." Slocum almost laughed when she tossed the poor lizards to the ground and watched them race off. "We're going to ride another hundred yards—then get the gold."

"The gold? You've seen it?"

"I've found the last canyon going up to it. But we've got to ride hard and fast. There's not much time." He didn't tell her Magee was close behind or that the Indians ahead were blocking the way.

"The gold," she said, her eyes lighting up with an inner fire. Tiredness was forgotten. The lure of gold gave renewed strength to her limbs. She tugged at her horse and forced it to start walking again.

As Slocum followed, he wondered how they were ever going to get the gold out of the canyon. His map didn't show the details inside the box canyon, but even if there wasn't a trail to the rim their horses would never be able to carry much of the gold. They were too tired from the pursuit over the last four days.

"Here, John, is this the place?" The rugged crevice where Evangeline had stopped was hardly large enough for a horse and rider to squeeze into.

"Go on," he said. "Keep moving as fast as you can

and I'll join you in a few minutes. I've got to lay a false trail.''

She eyed him, as if doubting that he'd do any such thing.

"Very well," she said. "Give me the map, however."

He handed it over to her. There wasn't any reason not to. They were close enough to sniff the scent of riches.

He watched Evangeline slip into the narrow gorge. She looked over her shoulder once, gave him a curious half-smile and then hurried on. Slocum had no more time to wonder what she might be up to. She was one fine looking woman, but she was also a double-dealer.

Slocum climbed onto his tired horse and made as broad a trail as he could down the gravelly center of the canyon. He even went so far as to toss his hat into a mound of prickly pear cactus, as if it had blown off and he hadn't wanted to retrieve it. When his crude trail-laying was done, he got off and hacked some greasewood from the ground. He tied it behind the horse and led the animal back to the narrow opening in the canyon wall. The trail ought to send Quentin Magee and his men right into the arms of the Cheyenne war party.

If it didn't, they would at least be aware of one another and spend the rest of the day running back and forth like chickens with their heads cut off. Slocum just wanted both groups occupied to the point that they forgot about him and Evangeline for a spell.

He wiped the sweat from his forehead with his dusty bandanna and then hurried after the woman. He caught up with her about a half mile into the winding ravine.

"You came back," she said, almost startled.

"I told you I was laying a false trail. By the time they figure out what I did, we ought to have the gold and be long gone."

She smiled and Slocum felt the warmth of the sun on him. He looked at the sky to be sure the sun hadn't circled around in the sky and come back. It hadn't. The warmth was from Evangeline and Evangeline alone. It had been a while since she had showered him with such a fine look, and Slocum wasn't sure if he didn't like it. A lot. She might be a crook, an adulteress, and a conniving bitch, but he knew that and it didn't seem to matter much to him at the moment.

"What if there isn't any gold?" she asked.

"What if there is?" Slocum countered. "How are we going to get it out of here? It must have taken a year to get anything down this tight pass." His shoulders brushed the sides of the ravine at times. The heat was stifling in the stony prison, but he kept moving, glad that the sun had passed its zenith.

"Look at this," she said, moving forward. "It's an oasis. A little drop of paradise in a terrible world."

"If nothing else, this is worth it," Slocum said. A waterfall tumbled from a hundred feet above into a deep, clear pool. Surrounding the water was a small grove of cottonwoods. Grass grew in abundance for the horses. Slocum let them go to graze. It might take a few days for them to regain their strength, but amid such forage it would happen.

"There's even fish in the pond," Evangeline said in glee. "We don't have to eat those horrible lizards."

"Paradise," Slocum agreed. He started walking around, thinking how good a bath would feel. The treasure map hadn't shown this. He guessed that the entire area had to be on the lost half of the map.

"What is it, John? You have that far-off look in your eye again."

"What's that under the waterfall?"

"Nothing. A big dark circle. A cave?"

"A cave big enough for Spanish gold," he said. He shucked off his boots and waded across the edge of the pond to a rocky ledge behind the waterfall. He slipped and almost fell on the slime-covered rock worn smooth by centuries of falling water. Evangeline crowded him from behind.

"Go on. Don't stop now. I want to see!"

Slocum took a deep breath. There might not be any gold. It may have been taken out of this cave years back. Or the gold might not even exist. Fake treasure maps were bought and sold all the time. He moved into the cave, bent over because of the low ceiling.

When he dropped to his knees, though, it was because of what he had found.

"John," Evangeline Dunbar whispered as if in church for a service, "can it be real?"

"It is," he said. "The whole damned cave's chock full of gold!"

17

"It's a gold coin," Slocum said, picking it up and biting down on one smooth edge. The softness told him it was almost pure gold. It was far bigger than any double eagle he had ever seen. Five times the size, it had to be worth a young fortune—and it was just one of a large box of the coins.

"It's a Spanish doubloon," Evangeline said. "I've heard about them. They used to cut them into eight pieces and each piece was still valuable."

"There's enough here to keep us happy for a long time," Slocum said. He settled back and stared at the box of gold coins. There must be five thousand dollars' worth of gold right here, and it was all easily carried out of the small box canyon. He couldn't have asked for a more perfect ending to this treasure hunt.

"You thought it was all a myth, didn't you, John?"

"I have to admit it," he said honestly. "I didn't believe

it would be here." He started rummaging through the box and a few of the coins spilled into the muck on the floor. He picked up the first few he dropped, then noticed there were dozens more that he hadn't dropped. He began sweeping away the mud and found almost as many as were in the worm-eaten, rotten wood box.

"There's more?" Evangeline crowded past him and worked her way deeper into the cave. On hands and knees she began following the golden trail leading back from the waterfall.

"Be careful," Slocum said. "There might be a booby trap. Or the roof might cave in on you."

"Booby trap?" she scoffed. "Why bother leaving this box out in plain sight if you're going to booby-trap the cave deeper into the mountain? And the cave's been here for years. There's no reason for it to pick right now to collapse."

Slocum wasn't so sure. The action of the water was gradual but still pervasive. The rocky sides dripped constantly, hinting that the roof wasn't too secure.

"John!" The woman's voice choked with excitement.

"What is it?"

"I'll trade you what I've just found for the box out there." The teasing note told him she had found something really tremendous.

"Let me see." He pushed beside her in the narrow cave for a better look. The light getting this far into the cave was almost too dim to see by, but the bright sparkles from the pile of gold plate was more than any darkness could dim.

"I don't believe this. There must be a hundred pounds of gold, just in dinner plates."

"There's more," she said. "See?" Wiggling on her belly, Evangeline crowded past the heaps of gold plates and began digging in the mud. She had always complained about the dirt and stench on the trail. Not now. She scented pure

)ld and nothing was going to stop her. "There's more. I
vear, there's a pit filled with gold!"

Slocum watched in amazement as she began pulling up
ncy breastplate armor of solid gold, implements decorated
ith gold and just about any kind of bridle or gear for a
orse imaginable—all made from gold.

"We're rich, John, rich!"

"I want to see this in the daylight. There's some trick.
here must be. Nobody leaves this kind of wealth behind."

"The Indians do. That's the story. They stole all this
om the Spanish and then hid it. It might have been here
or two hundred years! Longer!"

"It's not gold," Slocum said. "It can't be."

It was. They began dragging out the armor, the plates
` pure gold, the boxes of Spanish coins—it was all pure
)ld. Slocum sat cross-legged behind the waterfall, wash-
g off the muck from the cave and using the tip of his
iife to scratch each and every piece. He expected to see
ise metal show. One or two of the coins had to be made
om gold-plated lead. There wasn't this much fortune in
l the world.

Every piece he checked showed only the brightest, shi-
est of metal. It was all gold.

"We *are* rich," he said in awe. "I never dreamed there'd
this much gold in the world, and it's all ours!"

He sat with his feet in the water and a solid gold breast-
ate in his hands. He examined the exquisite workmanship,
it it was the bulk of the relic that appealed to him.

"You don't know how to use that, do you, John? Here,
t me see it."

He handed her the breastplate. She quickly skinned off
er wet clothing, thrust her head under the falling water for
moment to get the last of the mud off her hair, and then,
aked except for the Spanish armor she held in front of her
est, strutted around.

"You're quite a sight. Any conquistador would give up
s armor—and his honor—for you."

"You like it?" she teased. Evangeline tossed back her head and let her long, brunette hair cascade down her back. She held the gold armor more modestly, lowering it a little to hide the damp, fleecy, chestnut-colored triangle between her legs. Then she let out a yelp as her feet slipped out from under her. She thrashed about as she tumbled through the water and splashed into the pool.

"Help me, John. I can't swim with the gold."

"Don't try," he said, laughing. "There's more where that came from."

"I'm serious. Help me!"

Her head vanished under the water. He experienced a moment's fear that she might have gotten entangled in some underwater growth. Slocum dived cleanly through the water and splashed into the pond beside her. He took in a gulp of air and submerged, intending to see if she had gotten tangled. He found only sleek white legs gently kicking just below the surface. The bottom of the pool here was carved deep from years of falling water, but there was a smooth ledge only a few feet behind Evangeline.

"Back," he said, treading water. "Move back a ways and you can stand up on the bottom."

She rolled onto her back and kicked powerfully. Holding the Spanish breastplate over her, she looked like a golden turtle moving through the water. But Slocum had never seen such a beautiful turtle in all his life.

When Evangeline found the rocky bottom, she stood, still clinging to the armor.

"I didn't want to lose it," she said.

Slocum swam slowly to her and got his feet under him. He stood, his body pressing into hers. Her wide brown eyes locked with his green ones. She let the golden armor slip from her hands and fall to the bottom of the watery hollow. Lips parting slightly, she closed her eyes and tilted her head back.

Slocum remembered how she had double-crossed just about everyone she'd ever had dealings with, but it didn' matter to him at that moment. There was more than enough gold for the both of them—and he desired her. He felt himself responding. If anything, the nearness of such immense riches acted as a powerful aphrodisiac for him. Bending over, his lips met hers.

The kiss deepened. Evangeline's arms circled his neck and pulled him close. Then she broke off the passionate kiss and whispered hotly in his ear, "You're way overdressed. Take your clothes off and let them dry while we—"

"While we do what?" he goaded.

"We'll think of something," she said. Her tongue followed her tempting words into his ear. Then she wiggled it around, tormenting him as he tried to strip off his wet clothes. Slocum tossed the duds to the gravely beach and turned back to the woman.

"I've got a few ideas what we can do," he said.

"Really? It took you long enough." Evangeline smiled broadly and slid back into the water. As he reached for her, she slipped from his grip like a cavorting sea otter. Laughing, she splashed and tried to swim away. Slocum was too fast for her.

Grabbing, he caught her. Together they both sank under the cool surface of the water. Somehow their lips met and when they surfaced they were both sputtering for breath. Evangeline tossed her mane of russet hair from her face and stared at him.

He had never seen a more beautiful or desirable woman. A light kick carried him closer. Their bodies slid slickly across one another until they got themselves properly positioned. Evangeline's arms were around Slocum's neck and his arms tightened around her waist.

"Umm, I like what I feel," she said, wiggling her hips. He stiffened even more as her hips churned against his groin. "Are you going to do something about it?"

"Why not? We're rich and we have all the time in the world." Their lips met again, this time tongues dancing back and forth until they were both so hot they felt like exploding. The pressure mounting within Slocum was like floodwater behind a dam. It wouldn't be denied.

He floated onto his back and Evangeline came on top of him, her legs widening into a V as she moved. Easily, smoothly they merged into one. Then Slocum discovered that he couldn't breathe. His face kept going underwater. If he turned, Evangeline was the one unable to suck in enough air.

"Back a ways," she guided him. "There, right there. Yes!"

With his butt firmly resting on the smooth bottom of the pond Slocum was able to rear up enough to keep their bodies in the water and their heads in the air. It was perfect. Rocking to and fro caused waves to lap against their straining bodies, over them, caressing them in ways he hadn't thought possible. Evangeline began moving her hips back and forth until the friction mounted.

"More," she moaned out. "I need more, John. Don't deny me. Don't do it!"

He wasn't about to. His balls had tightened and felt like a powder keg ready to explode. Arching his back gave the woman the extra thrusting she so desperately desired. Together they flailed about in the pond with water droplets falling on them. Slocum thought they would cause the pond to boil with their passion.

The only explosion came from within. He tried to hold back but Evangeline was too beautiful, too demanding. Her hips levered back and forth and sucked him dry. He erupted into her yearning interior just as she threw back her head and let out a howl reminiscent of Sergeant Ben Madsen. The only difference was the cause. Her cry came from passion; his had come from madness.

Evangeline relaxed and rolled off Slocum. She paddled back into the center of the pond and then turned to face him. Her doelike brown eyes glistened and her broad smile captivated him all over again. This was a woman he could spend a considerable amount of time with and never get bored.

"Again, John? Shall we do it again? The first time was good. The next can be even better."

He was willing. He got his feet under him and started to kick off to capture the woman once more when he heard sounds from down the narrow canyon. Slocum stood up in the pool buck naked, water dripping from his body. It was getting toward twilight and the light wind sent shivers across his flesh.

"What's wrong, John?"

"Get dressed. We've got company on the way."

"Damnation," Evangeline cried. "I thought you took care of them!"

"There's no telling who's coming to visit. It might be Magee or it might be the Cheyenne war party. Whoever won the skirmish out in the canyon must have decided to come looking for us."

Even as he pulled on his clothing, he knew who had entered the narrow canyon. It had to be Quentin Magee. There hadn't been enough Indian braves to fight off Magee's men. And when he had finished with the Cheyenne party, Magee had come looking for his quarry. It was obvious Slocum and Evangeline hadn't slipped past the Indians. That could only mean they'd sneaked off down a branching canyon.

This one was the only possible route. And Slocum had been too foolish to simply take the gold and be off. He didn't know how they were going to escape from this trap. If Magee had more than three or four men left, he could drive a deadly cork in the neck of the canyon that would bottle Slocum up forever.

"It might be the Indians," Evangeline said, shaking herself dry like a dog and then climbing into her clothing. Slocum wanted to watch the lovely woman dress. The sight of the bare limbs vanishing was as tantalizing this way as it was when she slipped off her garments. But there wasn't time. No time, no time.

Slocum looked around for a way out of the trap. They might get lucky. It might be the Indians come to water their horses. If so, they wouldn't go into the cave. It must be a holy site for them. But Slocum knew even this wouldn't work. The Cheyenne would see their horses and come looking for them. Holy site or not, the cave wasn't entirely off limits in matters of desecration.

And he had to admit the cave was a terrible place to be caught. There wasn't any way out if he and Evangeline went inside. A trap within a trap.

"John, the map. See this line? I think it might mean there's a trail up the side of the canyon."

He glanced from the half of the map Evangeline had spread out to the south wall. There was a chance they might be able to make it up the trail—if it even existed. The map had been creased and stained over the past few weeks. The trail she pointed out might not even exist.

"We don't have a lot of choice," he said. "Start getting the gold coins out. Leave the heavy armor and gold plates. The horses would never be able to carry that much of a load up these steep canyon walls. We can always come back for the rest later."

"No!" He heard greed in the woman's swift denial. "Quentin won't leave us a speck of gold!"

"Then we'd better take what we can and get out of here. Your precious Quentin will leave us for buzzard bait. He's not going to let us walk out of here with so much as a memory of the gold."

Evangeline hesitated, thinking hard. She came to some conclusion he couldn't understand. The windows of her lovely brown eyes had become closed to him.

"I'll get the coins," she said. "As much as we can carry up the slope."

"Hurry!"

Slocum strapped on his gun belt and checked his Winchester. They might have to fight their way out of this trap. He didn't have any illusions about that result. He would die in the worst way possible. He would die rich without getting the chance to spend any of the gold.

18

"Get on up the canyon," he ordered Evangeline. Slocum watched as the woman worked to fill the saddlebags on the horses with as much gold as she could. He worried that she overloaded them. The two animals had rested a mite, but they were still tired from the frantic four days of riding it had taken to get to this secluded canyon and the cave filled with Spanish gold. The only consolation Slocum could see was that Quentin Magee's men weren't any more rested after the chase. Their mounts would be tuckered out, too.

"But John, the rest of the gold. There's a fortune in that cave! It's ours! We've earned it!"

"We can get it later," he said. He knew he was lying. No matter what happened, they would never be back. Either Magee would get it when they left or they'd be dead and in no condition to return for the hundreds and hundreds of pounds of the yellow metal still resting in the muck on the cave floor.

Evangeline started up the hidden trail at the edge of the grove. He saw her horse stumble once. She dismounted and made better time. He checked his rifle again and knew he was in for one hell of a fight. Before he could even find a place to make his stand, a bullet came whistling through the air.

Slocum dived forward and lay prone on the ground, firing slowly to make the most of his ammunition. In the gathering darkness, it was hard to find good targets. That didn't prevent him from winging one gunman. Slocum waited for the foot-long tongue of fire to jump from the other man's six-shooter and then aimed a few inches above it. Twice this trick worked.

"Damn, he can see in the dark!" came a loud protest.

"He's firing at your muzzle flash," came Quentin Magee's cold words. "Calm down and go ferret out that son of a bitch. I want him. And I want him *bad*."

Slocum heard a cocking of rifles as all of Magee's men began preparing for the assault. There weren't many of them left, but Magee had them well under control. They weren't likely to make any serious mistakes Slocum could capitalize on. Slocum knew he couldn't stay where he was much longer. He rolled and kept rolling until he came to where his horse nervously stirred, spooked by the action. When the volley of hot lead cut loose, Slocum thought he was going deaf. They had fired a perfectly timed barrage. All Magee's men cocked and fired again simultaneously, the thunder of the report shaking the ground.

Slocum dropped to one knee, wondering if he had been hit. Then he realized the ground was moving. He gathered his wits and understood the real source of the ominous sound. The deep rumble came from behind the waterfall. The cave with the gold had collapsed from the cacophony of the heavy rifle fire being focused down the narrow ravine. The sound had worked where centuries of wind and dripping water had not to bring down the muddy cave's roof.

Slocum watched the dust and mud billow from the mouth

of the cave. Most of the debris was swallowed by the falling water. He knew he couldn't stay much longer. Magee would get the idea to charge. Slocum had to be on his way up the side of the cliff before that happened. Thanking his lucky stars that the trail was real and not just a spurious line on the treasure map, he grabbed the reins and jerked his nervous horse behind him. The animal balked. Slocum was in no mood to be gentle. His life depended on the horse obeying.

He fired his rifle immediately behind the animal's tail. The horse jumped straight into the air when the hot powder singed its tail. Slocum took advantage of the movement to get into the saddle. He stayed low as the horse took off.

Behind him, toward the waterfall and the dancing shadows it cast, Magee's men concentrated their fire. The waves of thunder deafened Slocum now. But he saw the hint of a trail starting up the side of the cliff. His horse never broke stride as they got to the rocky slope and began up. The horse started stumbling a few yards up. Only then did Slocum dismount and lead the horse.

"They're around here somewhere. Dammit, do not let them escape," came Magee's precise, clipped words. "I will double the reward for the man—dead. And triple it for Evie—alive."

Slocum knew where he stood with the San Francisco peacock. The man was willing to pay handsomely to get the woman back and put Slocum six feet under. He continued up the side of the mountain until he got fifty yards along the trail. From this vantage point, he could see the dark shadows moving through the narrow gorge. A few well-placed shots would cut down Magee's men. But Slocum held his fire. They hadn't found the trail leading out of the ravine yet. Slocum wanted to keep it that way. There would be plenty of time later to set a proper ambush if they tried following.

Slocum almost relished the thought of being on the rim of the canyon and potshotting each of the men as they struggled to the top along this narrow trail.

The commotion in the valley increased when one man found the discarded golden Spanish breastplate. Magee roared and the men went crazy with greed. All pretense of discipline flew away. Slocum kept moving doggedly, never looking back down the constricted trail but still listening to what went on below him. By the time he reached the top of the cliff, he was exhausted. His horse repeatedly slipped and was close to collapsing.

But he was on top of the cliff and Magee's men were still in the secluded cul de sac trying to find the golden treasure.

Slocum hadn't expected Evangeline Dunbar to wait for him when she got to the canyon rim. It came as quite a surprise when he looked around on the narrow finger of rock that formed this part of the canyon verge and saw her sitting patiently on a low boulder. She smiled and held something out for him.

"What is it?" he asked. He couldn't quite make it out in the dim twilight.

"Dinner," she said. She had caught another blue-tailed lizard.

"Won't he *ever* give up?" Evangeline cried in exasperation. "I swear, that man will be the death of me."

For two days they had been working their way through the mountains, cutting back across their trail and hurrying on in a vain attempt to lose Magee and his men. Slocum wasn't quite sure when Magee had discovered their elementary ruse and come after them again, but for the past six hours Magee and four of his men had been within a mile and intent on cutting down the distance with every passing hour. They were clever enough not to try to put on one intense burst of speed which would tire their mounts rapidly. Magee was inching closer, his horses stronger and faster by a hair.

"The gold's slowing us down," Slocum said. Close to twenty pounds of gold rode slung over the hindquarters of his horse. A similar amount now weighed down Evangeline's.

"I will *not* give it up," she said firmly. "I've been through hell for it. And so has William."

She looked at him and a firmness set her jaw into a rigid line. "I know what you're trying to do. You want it all. It's not enough having your own saddlebags filled. You want my gold, too."

"It's not like that, Evangeline," said Slocum. He was too tired to argue with her. In truth, the idea had never crossed his mind. He was toying with the idea of burying his share somewhere and coming back to retrieve it when Magee wasn't so hot on their trail. With Magee and his henchmen close behind, though, there wasn't any chance he could do it.

"Then think of some way of getting rid of Quentin. I refuse to give up my gold."

Slocum looked around and tried to picture where they were. Desolation Point and the fort weren't more than fifteen miles behind them. He knew they'd never be able to get back to Fort Desolation, even if they wanted. Slocum saw no need. The only protection in the fort came from Ben Madsen, and he wouldn't be able to keep Magee from filling them full of holes to get the gold.

But as Slocum thought about the crazy man, a harebrained scheme began to form. He hadn't seen any sign of the Cheyenne for two days, but that didn't mean they weren't around.

"Keep an eye peeled for the Indians," Slocum told Evangeline. "We can use them right about now."

"What? Have you gone mad? They'd scalp us in an instant!"

Slocum was past trying to explain his reasoning to the woman. She was tired and suspicious and ready to explode in all directions. The best he could do was keep them alive and maybe get to Cedar City and from there to civilization.

The gold wasn't going to do either of them any good out here in the wilderness.

He kept riding, alert for sign of the Cheyenne war party. He found it less than an hour later—just in time. Quentin Magee had closed the gap between them, and Slocum heard the man shouting orders to his henchman. In another few miles Magee would overtake them.

"Do exactly as I say," Slocum told the woman. "Do it and we might get out of this alive and with the gold. So much as hesitate and you're a goner. Do you understand?"

"What are you—"

"Do you understand?" He looked behind him. Magee was whipping his horse into a lather to catch them. He would reach them before they could do anything significant to get away.

"Yes," Evangeline said sullenly. He could tell she wasn't happy about having to obey without cross-examining him. Slocum would never have told her the details of his plan because it wasn't something she could think about and carry out. If she knew what he was up to, she'd get cold feet at the crucial instant.

"Ride like your tail's on fire," he said, "and shoot at anything that moves that's not me. Whatever you do, stay low and don't stop. Keep riding. You got that?"

"Yes, but—"

"Then ride!"

He put his heels to his horse's flanks. The horse responded with a surge of speed. Slocum slid his Colt Navy from its cross-draw holster and cocked the pistol. He let loose the first round the instant he saw the Cheyenne standing sentry duty. The bullet missed by a country mile but still drove the Indian to cover. He kept his heels kicking at his horse and rode through the center of the Cheyenne's main camp. Slocum didn't even try to count; there must have been two dozen braves sitting around campfires.

He fired steadily. He might have killed one warrior. He wasn't sure, and it didn't matter. He heard Evangeline firing her carbine. He also heard it jam. Looking back over his shoulder he saw her swing it and bring the barrel up smartly against a brave's temple. The Indian reeled back and fell into another.

"Keep riding!" shouted Slocum. He didn't need to encourage Evangeline. She was bent low and riding like the wind. In less than a minute they were both on the other side of the Cheyenne encampment—and Magee's men were just arriving.

The Cheyenne had been caught by surprise by Slocum and Evangeline, but they were ready to fight when Magee exploded into the center of their camp. It sounded as if a small war had broken out. Once more the Cheyenne fought Magee. This time he didn't have Fort Desolation to protect him.

"My god, John, they'll kill Quentin!"

"Probably," Slocum said, pulling his horse back from its headlong gallop. Another few minutes of this and the animal would have died under him. "But I think it's better that they scalp him than us."

Evangeline rode alongside him for a few minutes, her knee occasionally brushing his. She finally said, "And I certainly did not want to give over my share of the gold to Quentin." She smiled wickedly. "He got what he deserved, didn't he?"

Slocum didn't bother to answer. He was alive and his saddlebags were filled with Spanish gold. That was enough for him.

19

"I can't remember ever being this tired, John." Evangeline Dunbar forced herself to keep awake as they rode along. "I'm hot, I'm tired, I'm hungry and thirsty, and I want to sleep for a million years."

Slocum reflected on the gold riding in their saddlebags and how little good it had done them over the past few days. The Cheyenne war party had removed Quentin Magee from their trail once and for all. Slocum didn't know if Magee was dead or alive, and it didn't much matter to him. He had taken a dislike to the San Francisco dandy the instant he had set eyes on him. Slocum tried to figure out if this was because of the way the foppish man ordered his henchman around, the way he had looked with his fine mustache and fancy clothing—or that he had been sleeping with Evangeline.

Slocum finally decided it didn't matter a whole lot. He hadn't liked him, and Magee was probably dead.

Too many were dead. Cheyenne warriors, troopers, Magee's men—too many had died during the past few weeks. And he and Evangeline were the only ones to get any part of the Spanish gold. Even her husband William had died. It had been one hell of a long and bloody road to the Spanish gold from that night of incautious gambling in the Union Club back in San Francisco.

"We're getting there," Slocum said.

"Where's that?"

Slocum pointed. A crudely lettered sign proclaimed the town ahead to be Cedar City. At the sight of promised civilization Evangeline perked up. By the time they rode into the sleepy little town, she was alert and ready for anything.

"John, look, there *is* a railroad! They lied to us about there not being one."

He shook his head. "When we asked, there wasn't one." He recognized the crew foreman he had spoken to outside Fort Desolation. The man and his track laying crew had been working day and night to get this much done. The steel rails vanished over a low pass toward the north.

"See you're eyein' our fancy railroad," a man said from the porch of the general store. "Don't reckon it's gonna be acceptin' passengers for a good long while."

"Why's that?" Slocum asked.

"They're just now getting around to connecting with the line from Salt Lake City. Grand opening's not supposed to happen for another week or two. Course in this town, any damned thing's cause for celebratin'."

"You're not happy with the railroad coming to town?"

"Not happy with anything that changes the way it is. Cedar City's a fine place without the 'road. Can't see how it's gonna improve the town once it starts bringing all them city folk."

Slocum kept from laughing. He didn't know what there was this close to Desolation Point to bring in the railroad, but he was glad it was here. Even waiting a week or two would be better than having to ride back across the desert to Elko or even Salt Lake City itself.

"John, there's a rooming house. I'll check to see if there's a room we can rent."

"Go on, Evangeline," he said, distracted. "I'll catch up in a few minutes."

She eyed him strangely and then turned her horse toward the small house with the white picket fence and the small sign giving daily and weekly rates.

Slocum dismounted and went to a small construction shack by the side of the tracks. Inside, the foreman labored over some paperwork. He chewed his tongue as he painstakingly wrote out a report on his crew for the home office. He looked up when Slocum blocked the light coming through the doorway.

"It's you," he said after a moment of trying to place Slocum's face. "Didn't expect to ever see you again. Thanks for steering us away from the damned redskins. The whole place is filthy with them. That's the last time I ever hire a scout hanging around a city."

"Tell me about the train," Slocum said, settling down to listen.

"Don't bother unpacking," Slocum told Evangeline. "The train's going to be here any minute."

"But the man at the store said it wouldn't be here for weeks and weeks."

"Grab your gold and come on," he repeated. "I sweet-talked the construction foreman into getting a place on the supply train. It's not as fancy as a passenger car but it'll drop off supplies and be back in Salt Lake by noon tomorrow."

"Noon?" Evangeline let out a deep sigh. "You mean I'll be able to see real people again?"

"You'll be able to get a room at the finest hotel in town, get a hot bath, eat the finest food—whatever you want."

"Let's go," she said, dragging the heavy saddlebags off

the bed. "When we get to Salt Lake City, I'll treat you to the finest meal you ever had."

"Hurry, Evangeline, there's the train now." Slocum looked out the front window of the boarding house and saw greasy black plumes of smoke rising from the makeshift train station. Together they went to the rude platform.

"Glad to see you made it, Slocum," said the foreman. "The turnaround time's been cut. We needed to bring more track and they screwed up the order. I'm sending the train straight back to fetch it, less I miss my deadline."

The foreman eyed Evangeline with some appreciation. She clutched the saddlebags with her gold tightly and moved closer to Slocum.

"Don't worry, Evangeline," Slocum said. "This is going to work out for the best. Let me help you up."

"It's not a proper train," she said, eyeing the small car with some distaste. She climbed up and looked around, then turned back and exclaimed, "John, there's hardly room for me here. This car's still loaded."

"We got to move back some of our construction equipment. They need it on another branch going northwest from Salt Lake and we're finished with it here and over at Mule Head City," the foreman said. "You won't be troubled none by the load shifting."

"And there's no need for space for both of us," Slocum finished for the man. "I'll be staying on for a while."

"What? Wait, John. Why?"

"It's for the best, Evangeline. We both know it." He stepped up and gave her a quick, unsatisfying kiss. The engine began grinding its steel wheels against the new track and snorting plumes of sooty smoke. "Our paths might cross one day."

"John, wait, no!"

Evangeline hung in the door of the tightly packed car unsure what to do. By the time a decision had been reached the train was moving too fast for her to jump off.

Slocum watched her vanish around a curve. The stea

engine strained and belched and gained speed for the long and arduous haul up the steep grade into the mountains. And for a long time after the train had slipped behind the mountains he kept watching and wondering if he had done the right thing.

He finally turned and walked off, secure in his knowledge that sending Evangeline Dunbar on her way had been the right thing for him. She was a lovely woman, but she was a two-timing, double-crossing woman—maybe the worst kind of bitch a man could find. She was a lightning rod for trouble he could do without. Let her spend her gold however she saw fit.

He would find somewhere else to spend his, somewhere without Evangeline Dunbar.

WESTERNS!

at least a savings of $3.00 each month below the publishers price. Second, there is never any shipping, handling or other hidden charges—Free home delivery. What's more there is no minimum number of books you must buy, you may return any selection for full credit and you can cancel your subscription at any time. A TRUE VALUE!

Mail the coupon below

To start your subscription and receive 2 FREE WESTERNS, fill out the coupon below and mail it today. We'll send your first shipment which includes 2 FREE BOOKS as soon as we receive it.

Mail To:
True Value Home Subscription Services, Inc.   12615-X
P.O. Box 5235
120 Brighton Road
Clifton, New Jersey 07015-5235

YES! I want to start receiving the very best Westerns being published today. Send me my first shipment of 6 Westerns for me to preview FREE for 10 days. If I decide to keep them, I'll pay for just 4 of the books at the low subscriber price of $2.45 each; a total of $9.80 (a $17.70 value). Then each month I'll receive the 6 newest and best Westerns to preview Free for 10 days. If I'm not satisfied I may return them within 10 days and owe nothing. Otherwise I'll be billed at the special low subscriber rate of $2.45 each; a total of $14.70 (at least a $17.70 value) and save $3.00 off the publishers price. There are never any shipping, handling or other hidden charges. I understand I am under no obligation to purchase any number of books and I can cancel my subscription at any time, no questions asked. In any case the 2 FREE books are mine to keep.

Name _____

Address _____ Apt. # _____

City _____ State _____ Zip _____

Telephone # _____

Signature _____
(if under 18 parent or guardian must sign)
Terms and prices subject to change.
Orders subject to acceptance by True Value Home Subscription Services, Inc.

JAKE LOGAN
TODAY'S HOTTEST ACTION WESTERN!